8/16

THE
MINISTRY
OF GHOSTS

ALSO BY ALEX SHEARER:

The Cloud Hunters
Sky Run

THE MINISTRY OF GHOSTS

ALEX SHEARER

Sky Pony Press
NEW YORK

Sky Pony Press books may be purchased in bulk at special discounts for sales promotion, corporate gifts, fund-raising, or educational purposes. Special editions can also be created to specifications. For details, contact the Special Sales Department, Sky Pony Press, 307 West 36th Street, 11th Floor, New York, NY 10018 or info@skyhorsepublishing.com.

Sky Pony® is a registered trademark of Skyhorse Publishing, Inc.®, a Delaware corporation.

Visit our website at www.skyponypress.com.

10 9 8 7 6 5 4 3 2 1

Library of Congress Cataloging-in-Publication Data is available on file.

Cover Art Direction: Jet Purdie
Cover Design: Jan Bielecki
Cover Illustration: Victor Rivas

Print ISBN: 978-1-5107-0473-2
Ebook ISBN: 978-1-5107-0471-8

Printed in the United States of America

J
SHEARER
ALEX

If there are any—then for all of them

PROLOGUE

Some of the best and most interesting things in life are often right under your nose. Yet, you don't even notice them, for you are too busy looking elsewhere.

Perhaps many of you lose yourselves in daydreams of big adventures in faraway places, but fail to see the possibilities of what is just around the corner. Home, you may think, is a dull, everyday sort of place. Not much excitement there, just the same thing over and over again . . .

At least that was what young Thruppence Coddley thought, and her school friend Tim Legge, if asked, would no doubt have agreed with her.

Adventures were what you hoped to find on your vacations, on a desert island or up a mountain or in a forest or in a swamp. There would probably be a crocodile involved. You didn't think to find excitement and danger just down the road and around the corner, along a boring old street with drab buildings in it.

Yet, that is the great thing about adventures: they creep up on you softly and tap you on the shoulder when you least expect them.

"Excuse me, Thruppence," they say. "I've been looking for you."

"Pardon me, Tim," they whisper. "But have you got a minute?"

And startled, amazed, a little nervous, but expectant and excited, Thruppence Coddley would have said, "Hello. You're an adventure, are you? I'm glad to meet you then, as I've wanted one for quite some time."

As for Tim Legge, he'd have gripped that adventure tightly by the arm. "You're not getting away," he'd have told it. "You stay right there, and don't move. And don't talk to anybody else. You're mine."

Such is the way of adventures and of the people who have them. Some lucky people attract them, the way magnets attract bits of metal, and their lives are nothing but adventures, all the way to the end.

Maybe if one tapped you on the shoulder, too, you might not turn it away, either. Even if it scared you half to death.

As adventures often do.

Especially spooky ones.

1
BRIC-A-BRAC STREET

The Ministry of Ghosts was one of those obscure, unknown, tucked-away places that you only usually ever come across by accident, if you come across them at all.

If you were you looking for the Ministry of Ghosts, or making inquiries in that direction, the chances are that you would never find it. But if you were searching for somewhere else entirely, you might easily stumble across it, quite unexpectedly and out of the blue.

And then there you would be: looking with awe, maybe with bafflement, perhaps with incredulity and the feeling that some hoax—or trick—was being played on you, as you gazed at the unpolished and seriously tarnished nameplate by the door.

If you glanced to the windows, you would see cobwebs in their corners, long unbothered by draughts and feather dusters, as if inside were a vacuum of the undisturbed past.

On a summer's day, a sense of chill radiated out from the Ministry building, as if the place were a fridge. In winter, its offices seemed at one with the cold, bitter streets. It would be a hard place to keep warm in, you would think, as you wrapped your scarf around your neck and buttoned your coat tighter against the cold. And yet . . .

There was also something intriguing about the place; something that bade you to loiter, to scrutinize its elegant, if ancient, facade; something that drew you in; some curiosity that would have you lingering, peeking in through the dusty windows, pressing your nose to the cold glass in an effort to see inside.

But what would you see there in the Ministry of Ghosts? Not much, apparently. Not, at least, if that look through the front window was anything to go by.

There was just a big, uncomfortable-looking room, lined with obscure and seldom-read books: old, misshapen, leather-bound volumes, many with shabby spines that looked as though they would simply fall apart if opened. But others seemed as though they might never have been opened at all and could be just as pristine inside as on the day of their creation.

Some of those books were in Latin; some in other languages. Most were in English, but even then, often of an ancient and complicated kind, unfamiliar to a modern eye.

The more legible of the books bore curious titles. *Ghosts and How to Catch Them. A Ghost Catcher's Manual—Written by a Person of Great Experience. Poltergeists—Detection and Laying to Rest. Apparitions from the Other Side—by a Gentleman. Memoirs of a Lady Psychic.* And so on. Books written with a straight face and a fancy pen by authors who took themselves very seriously—and who expected their readers to do the same.

Yes, there were useful books on every aspect of ghosts, except on one particular point, for not one line in one paragraph of those dense and innumerable pages ever questioned whether ghosts actually existed. It was taken for granted that they did and that only a fool would think otherwise.

Because ghosts *had* to exist, or there was no point in the Ministry of Ghosts existing. And then those who worked there would be out of a job. Which would be highly inconvenient for them. So there was every reason and incentive for them to go on believing the unprovable and contestable assertion that ghosts were real.

Yet ghosts, like many other supernatural matters, are more items of faith than demonstrable fact. People of a logical mind tend not to believe in them; people of a more spiritual inclination often do.

Some people swear that they have seen them, felt their presence and proximity, been bothered by them, terrified by them, that ghosts have chucked their furniture about and flushed the toilet incessantly in the middle of the night. Others put these phenomena down to bad dreams brought on by eating cheese and pickle sandwiches before bedtime, or attribute them to magnetic and electrical forces or to overactive imaginations, or to watching the wrong movies. People say they've got ghosts in the attic or they're living in the faucet. But ninety-nine times out of a hundred, it just turns out to be bad plumbing or squirrels.

Yes, most people believe what suits them. Faith conquers reason. It often even boldly defies logic and plain common sense. Once, for instance, it was thought shocking to believe that the earth revolved around the sun, and not the other way around. Yet, now, thanks to astronomy, the fact cannot be denied.

But faith in the spiritual, or supernatural, also has another powerful enemy: money. Or rather, the lack of money and the necessity of paying one's way, of making ends meet, and of balancing the books.

And all this brings us now to a man clad in a drab suit and carrying a leather briefcase, who was currently making his way toward the Ministry of Ghosts on that Monday morning. He had a map and directions with him and so was unlikely to get lost.

His name was Franklin Beeston and, like the current occupants of the Ministry, he was a government employee, a civil servant no less. Franklin Beeston was neither young nor old, ugly nor handsome, fat nor thin. His briefcase contained a few official papers, but its main purpose was for the transportation of his lunch, which was sandwiches in a plastic, resealable container, and a thermos of tea (milk, no sugar). Mr. Beeston was not a man for cappuccinos and other such expensive extravagances. By making his own sandwiches and bringing his own tea, Mr. Beeston estimated that he was saving one thousand pounds a year in lunch money alone. No small sum, either. Not to a man with a family to support. Even though Mrs. Beeston also worked in the civil service and brought in a good salary of her own. Mr. Beeston took care of the pennies and the pounds, perhaps a little too much. But then, while his work was steady and secure,

his profession was not an occupation to grow rich in—
more one to remain contented in for the next thirty years
until he finally retired on a decent pension.

Mr. Beeston's department was "Cuts." That was not
its official name, but such was its purpose. It was there
to affect economies, to bring down unnecessary government expenditure, to reduce the burden on the taxpayer
and the public sector's wages bill. Politicians had made
promises, and had been elected on such promises and
now they were going to implement those promises, to
keep faith with their voters.

Significant cuts had been slated (for cuts, when
politicians speak of them, are always significant and
never anything less). Red tape was going to be slashed.
Dead wood was to be axed. Bureaucracy was to be reduced. Unnecessary expenditure was to be trimmed.
All government departments would need to "justify their existence" or they would be on the chopping
block. Redundancies would no doubt (sadly and re-
grettably) be inevitable, but necessary, for the public
good. Times were hard. It was an austerity budget, and
nothing would stand in its way.

Thus Mr. Beeston was heading for the Ministry of
Ghosts, to determine to what extent—if any—its continuing existence could be justified. If no justifications
could be made (and while not wishing to prejudge the
case, he thought it highly unlikely) then closure would be
inevitable. Those who worked in the Ministry of Ghosts
would be redeployed in less exciting and less esoteric
roles, or they would find themselves on the scrapheap.

Mr. Beeston did not consider it likely that those who had spent years working at the Ministry of Ghosts would find it easy to obtain or to adjust to alternative employment. Indeed, their past experience might even weigh against them. For Mr. Beeston was of the opinion that ghosts did not exist and never had.

"There are," he would tell anyone prepared to listen, "no ghosts. There never have been and never will be. There are people's imaginations, that's all. And ghosts are but figments of the imagination."

The Ministry was a relic of another age, he felt—one of those government agencies that had long since outlived its usefulness. It had become an irrelevance, an outmoded, outdated institution, along the lines of the Department of Horse-Drawn Vehicles or the Ministry for the Subjugation of the Colonies or the Department for the Inspection of Steam Engines.

Why the Ministry of Ghosts had not been closed down years ago was something of a mystery to Mr. Beeston. He could not think how its existence had ever been allowed to continue or how it had so long escaped the axe of financial constraint.

Maybe it was because the place was so well hidden and buried away, down a warren of narrow, antiquated streets full of buildings of equally antique appearance. It was like another world here, a place that time had forgotten. Here went on trades, which you might think had long been rendered obsolete. Here were small shops with weather-faded signs outside, boasting dates of origin going back hundreds of years. Deglemann and

Sons—Hatters and Milliners, for example. Or Spiegler & Co.—Sword Makers to the Gentry. Or Thoroughgood and Partners—Bespoke Tailors. Wortinbrass and Fanglewood—Shoe and Bootmakers and Stockists of Finest Spatterdashes. And Mrs. Runciward—Supplier of Ladies' Corsets, Whalebone Reinforcements a Speciality.

Yes, here, Mr. Beeston decided, as he made his way along the ever-narrowing alleyways, was, in a word, yesterday. This part of the city was the "yesterday" area. It reeked of nostalgia, of old-world charm, and equally, old-world discomforts. He even—hard as it was to believe—saw a horse-drawn cart pass by. It must have been a brewer's carriage, he thought, glancing at the old-fashioned lettering of the unfamiliar name, kept on as a public relations and advertising gimmick. Maybe it was stabled down here somewhere, and it trotted out every now and again to entertain the public and promote the sale of beer.

Mr. Beeston noted with distaste that the carthorse had left some droppings behind it. He stepped around the mess, on the one hand considering that it would be good for his tomato plants; on the other thinking that if dog owners had doggie bags then why didn't horse owners have horse ones?

Then he looked at his map again and, despite all his best efforts and logical dimensions, found himself slightly lost. He reoriented himself, turned to the left, and headed down Casement Way, which, he felt confident, would lead to Bric-a-Brac Street, and there he would find his fellow civil servants—colleagues in a way and yet strangers, too—at their desks and at their labors (were there any, and he doubted it) in the Ministry of Ghosts.

The horse and the carriage turned a corner and were gone with a clopping of hooves and a rattling of ironclad wheels.

Yet, the instant the cart disappeared from view, so did the sound of it vanish from earshot. Almost as if the cart had been an illusion, a figment of someone's imagination, or, perhaps, even an apparition—some kind of a hologram maybe, a specter, a trick of the light, even a ghost.

2
1792

Despite outward appearances of inactivity, the Ministry of Ghosts was a place of steady—if not exactly dynamic—endeavor. It ticked over like an idling engine, chugging steadily, even if not really going anywhere.

It was a minor establishment, as government ministries went, but that did not mean that paperwork was neglected or that the necessary forms were not completed in the appropriate manner with the prescribed color of ink. Far from it. Progress reports were issued—as required—every quarter, and annual appraisals were made every September.

The conduct of the staff was generally—even invariably—held to be satisfactory, often more than that. Sometimes it was ranked as exemplary, though it was hard to understand why. For the fact of the matter was that the Ministry of Ghosts, for all its plodding efforts, had not found a ghost, or produced any evidence for the existence of a ghost, in over two centuries. All they ever really had were their suspicions.

"They've done nothing that's useful in years!" Mr. Beeston had told his underlings back at the Economies Office.

"Yet they seem to be reasonably busy, sir," his assistant, Mrs. Peeve, said. "At least busier than the Ministry of Sleep Research—otherwise known as the Ministry of Nodding Off, of course."

"Seem to be busy. Say they're busy. But what do they actually *do*?"

"Well," Mrs. Peeve said, thumbing through some ancient papers marked "Articles of Establishment," "it appears that the Ministry of Ghosts was founded in seventeen ninety-two—"

"Seventeen ninety-two!" Mr. Beeston exclaimed. "I'm very surprised to hear that the place has been going so long—and achieving so little."

"I believe that back in the seventeen nineties, people were a little more open minded in some respects—"

"You mean gullible?" Mr. Beeston snorted.

"Certainly of a more inquiring nature, perhaps," Mrs. Peeve said. (For she had her own views on the matter of the afterlife, which she was not prepared to elaborate on in the presence of a cynic.) "After all, people had more open minds back then, as regards the supernatural, what with science still in its infancy and—"

"Well, it's grown up a bit since, hasn't it?" Mr. Beeston said.

"Do you think so, sir?"

"Indeed I do. Look what we have now—computers, the internet, planes, cars, space travel, smart phones, microwave ovens, smoothies—not that I buy them or any such extravagant refreshments. I save a fortune staying out of coffee places and juice bars. I

ALEX SHEARER

bring my own sandwiches and save at least a thousand a year."

"Good for you," Mrs. Peeve said—who had a daily latte herself.

Mr. Beeston reached over for the Articles of Establishment and read them through. The ancient, yellowing document had a ribbon in its lower corner, fastened in place by dried sealing wax. It had been signed with a flourish by some now long dead and—even back then—indecipherable hand.

The Ministry of Ghosts, the document read, *is hereby established under instruction of Parliament, for the investigation into the existence or otherwise of those paranormal bodies known in the vernacular as "ghosts." The duties and responsibilities of the Ministry of Ghosts will entail investigation, regular reportage of such investigations, and ultimately the reaching of a conclusion—one way or another—as to the existence of such paranormal entities and activity.*

It will further be within the responsibility and domain of said Ministry—should conclusive proof of such supernatural entities be found—to investigate the manner of their coming into being, the means of their continuing existence, their wants, needs, intentions, and purposes, their ultimate fate, and—in the case of bothersome ghosts—their possible eradication. (Subcontractors may be used in this field, subject to the usual approvals, competitive quotations, authorizations, and budgetary constraints.)

"Hmm," Mr. Beeston said. "So, the place was set up over two hundred years ago to find out if ghosts actually exist, and if so, how to get rid of them?"

"When they *need* getting rid of," Mrs. Peeve said. "I mean, if they aren't bothering you, why should you . . ." She lapsed into silence, aware that Mr. Beeston was regarding her with a disapproving eye. "That is," she picked up, determined not to be browbeaten by her superior, "live and let live."

"Maybe so," Mr. Beeston said. "Only ghosts aren't alive, are they? I thought they were supposed to be dead."

"Well, the people they belong to are certainly dead, I suppose," Mrs. Peeve said. "But maybe, in a sense, their ghosts . . . live on."

Mr. Beeston gave a snort. "It seems to me," he said, "that these people at this Ministry of Ghosts are onto a cushy little number and have been for quite some time. How many work there?"

"Four, I believe," Mrs. Peeve said, consulting the records. "Four plus a cat, as far as I can make out."

"A cat? You mean a cat is down as an employee?"

"Well. It's an expense," Mrs. Peeve said. "It keeps the mice down, apparently."

"And it gets paid for that?"

"No, but it gets a food and bedding allowance."

"Food and bedding!"

"And all vet fees paid."

"Extraordinary," Mr. Beeston said. "Why couldn't they just buy a mousetrap? Be an awful lot cheaper."

"You'd still have to buy the bait," Mrs. Peeve pointed out.

"Even so. Sheer extravagance, employing a cat. That cat'll be out on its ear if I have anything to do with it.

This is taxpayers' money we're responsible for. What would people think if they discovered that their money was going to cats?"

"It could be going to worse places," Mrs. Peeve muttered.

"So, who do we have working there?" Mr. Beeston asked. "Do we have a record? I assume we must."

"Well," Mrs. Peeve said, thumbing through the file, "apparently there used to be seventeen people working there."

"How many?!" Mr. Beeston demanded. "Seventeen? Seventeen people on full-time wages, just to find out whether or not ghosts exist!"

"Plus the cat, of course."

"Seventeen people and a cat! Sheer waste and extravagance!"

"But staffing numbers have been trimmed over the years," Mrs. Peeve told him. "So it says here. Apparently the staffing levels were intermittently reviewed, firstly in eighteen seventy-six, when they were reduced to twelve, then in nineteen sixteen, when they were reduced to four—"

"Probably the war effort," Mr. Beeston said.

"And have remained at that level since. Four plus the cat."

"Presumably not the same cat?" Mr. Beeston said.

"I imagine it would be more like a succession of cats," Mrs. Peeve said. "The staffing at the Ministry has now been at the same level for decades, comprising one senior civil servant, two junior, and a secretary."

"And a cat."

"That's right," Mrs. Peeve said.

"And in all that time and all those cats and all those people and all that money, what have they found?"

"One moment," Mrs. Peeve said, rummaging again through the file. "Ah, here we are. The quarterly progress reports."

"And?"

She flicked through them.

"It would appear that investigations are still under-way—"

"Huh!" Mr. Beeston gave vent to another of his snorts.

"But, as yet, no firm conclusions have been reached one way or the other."

"Let me see that!"

Mr. Beeston took the file and spun it around.

"There are several other boxes down in the archives," Mrs. Peeve said. "If you want to see them. In longhand, some of them. Dating right back to the seventeen nineties."

"No, thank you," Mr. Beeston said, picking up the most recent report, which despite its relative newness already seemed be impregnated with the odor of must and decay. "Four quarterly reports for over two hundred years—there must be nearly a thousand of them down there."

"True," Mrs. Peeve said. "If the rats and beetles haven't eaten a few."

"All saying the same thing, too, no doubt. That investigations are 'ongoing,' that evidence is 'being collected,' that the results are 'being weighed up and considered,' and that 'conclusive proof one way or the other is still lacking—but being diligently pursued.' You know what they're doing at this so-called Ministry of Ghosts, Mrs. Peeve?"

"What is that, sir?"

"They're joking. That's what they're doing. They're swinging the leash. They're pulling a fast one. They've got themselves a nice little cushy number and they're hoping it'll go on forever, until they can retire on handsome pensions after a life spent on a wild goose chase—"

"More of a wild ghost—"

"Ghost chase, goose chase, same difference, Mrs. Peeve. These characters are taking the taxpayer for a ride, and it's time it stopped. Because if you can't prove, after two hundred years' worth of investigations, that ghosts are real then there's only one possible conclusion."

"And what is that, sir?"

"They're not real. They don't exist. They're all in people's heads."

"But what about—?"

"Yes, yes. I know all about people who swear they've seen them, Mrs. Peeve. I also know people who swear they've seen flying saucers and that they've been abducted by aliens. The sad and the deluded are always with us. But I tell you this—these slackers and time wasters won't be at the Ministry of Ghosts for much longer. I'm going to issue an ultimatum, and then I shall shut the place down."

"But sir—"

"Oh, I shall be following the proper procedures, Mrs. Peeve, don't you worry about that. I shall be doing it by the book—by every letter of the book. I shall give them their chance to justify their continuing existence, and when they fail to do it, which I have no doubt they will, then the department will be closed down and they can be redeployed to more productive work."

"Yes, sir."

"Four civil servants, plus a cat, plus cost of premises, heating, lighting—we could easily save the taxpayers hundreds of thousands, Mrs. Peeve. If not millions—or at least that's what the costs could mount up to if this is allowed to go on."

"Yes, sir."

"We must all tighten our belts, Mrs. Peeve, and pull up our suspenders."

"I don't actually wear—"

"First thing next week, I shall commence my investigation."

"Yes, sir."

"I'll need to start by visiting the place, obviously."

"Yes, sir. Would you wish me to let them know . . . ?"

"Let them know I'm coming? Give them a chance to look busy? Certainly not. I shall turn up unannounced and unexpected. I shall probably catch them all napping—if they're there at all—and find the cat idling on a cushion somewhere. No, Mrs. Peeve, stealth and surprise are our weapons here in the Economies Office. I shall go there first thing next Monday morning and see what they're up to. And if I discover that they aren't up to anything at all and are just sitting there drinking tea and doing the crossword, then the fur shall fly, Mrs. Peeve. Rest assured of that. The fur shall most definitely fly! And that includes the cat."

"Yes, sir. Is that all for now?"

"Yes, you can take those files away for the moment, thank you."

Mrs. Peeve did as asked and carted the files back to the archive. As she left her superior's office, she heard the sound of a final snort.

"Ghosts, indeed!" Mr. Beeston said disparagingly. "Ghosts. I never heard such nonsense. Not in all my life."

Mrs. Peeve walked away, wondering if perhaps Mr. Beeston was right after all. Maybe there were no such things as ghosts. Maybe there was no spirit world, just the overwrought imaginations of the living and their desire to see their lost loved ones again, even if only fleetingly, as wraiths in the night or as tremulous mirages, briefly glimpsed in the shimmering heat haze of some sunny afternoon.

3

THE ART OF LOOKING BUSY

Four civil servants and a cat.

The cat was called Boddington. He lived half his life in the basement and the rest of it out in the streets. For he had his own cat door and could come and go as he pleased.

Although Boddington was—at least theoretically and technically—employed to keep the mouse population down, his activities in this area were meager and casual, and usually inconclusive.

It is possible that his presence deterred mice from lingering, but Boddington rarely caught any, seldom chased any, and—due to a congenital eye defect and the effects of age—seldom saw any. While he occasionally got the smell of them, it wasn't usually pungent enough to rouse him from his constant slumbers—it being in the nature of cats to spend most of their lives asleep.

Moving up the hierarchy of employees to the very top, the most senior of those engaged to run the Ministry of Ghosts with efficiency, was old Mr. Copperstone. Not that he was ever called "old" to his face. He was simply known as old Mr. Copperstone to his underlings—and usually when they and he were not in the same room. Old

Mr. Copperstone was of an ancientness that spoke of missed opportunities for retirement and of major slipups around at the Personnel Office (or Human Resources Office, as it was now known). Not only did Mr. Jeremiah Copperstone look ancient, he dressed the part, too, with stiff, starched collars, with cufflinks in his sleeves, with a suit of antique cut, and with an overcoat that could have been taken from a costume museum. Then there was his bowler hat and his furled umbrella, which never seemed to be unfurled, not even at times of rain. And then there was his antique leather briefcase, with his name in faded gold lettering upon it: J. J. COPPERSTONE, ESQUIRE. The case had seen good service, as had Mr. Copperstone, and both were old and faded now. Yet it was the work that kept him going. If old Mr. Copperstone hadn't had his work at the Ministry of Ghosts, he would scarcely have known what to do with himself; he would have been quite bereft.

Next in command was Miss Rolly. Miss Virginia Rolly was a woman not in the first flush of youth, but arguably still in youth's second flush, and her complexion matched her situation, being also very flushed, as though she were permanently embarrassed—which she was not, for Miss Rolly was as good as unembarrassable.

Miss Rolly just had one of those countryside kind of complexions that seemed the result of the outdoor life: of strong winds and severe temperatures and gales blowing up the estuary. Yet that was misleading, too, for Miss Rolly was a product of the suburbs and the inner city. She had been the first in her family to go to college, and she was a strong-minded woman and a staunch feminist.

"We must never give up the fight for women's rights. Eternal vigilance is the price of freedom," she sometimes asserted, and it was undoubtedly true. Miss Rolly had come up through the ranks of the civil service to head her own department at a relatively young age. True, the department was small, and the only other person in it—junior to and answerable to Miss Rolly—was one Mr. Arnold Gibbings.

The Ministry's general secretary, Mrs. Olive Scant, was really in a department of her own—not to say a world of her own. Mrs. Scant had her own little room at the end of a long hall, and here, when not typing out documents or firing off letters or dealing with telephone inquiries and "putting you through now," she spent quiet moments reading romantic novels, in which ladies of a certain age finally found the men of their dreams—having first suffered considerable heartache and having encountered several unsuitable types with big moustaches and dishonorable intentions along the way.

In terms of titles, old Mr. Copperstone was Ministry of Ghosts (Head of); Miss Rolly was Ministry of Ghosts, Detection and Executive Department (Head of); Mr. Gibbings was Ghost Liaison and Counseling Officer (and Assistant to Miss Rolly); and Mrs. Scant was Secretary to the above. Boddington was, presumably, Cat to the above. But his formal title had never been written down, so his exact status was unspecified. In the monthly petty cash expenditure, he was simply listed as "Cat."

A typical day at the Ministry of Ghosts would be as follows:

First Mr. Copperstone would appear in his office—for, as he was the most senior in rank, he felt it his duty to set a good example and high standards through punctuality, even earliness.

Next, invariably arriving almost together, but somehow not quite, Miss Rolly and Mr. Gibbings would enter their offices. They would exchange small talk and pleasantries regarding the weather then they would sit at their desks and deal with such paperwork as had come in.

There was often no paperwork at all, in which case Miss Rolly would delegate Mr. Gibbings to undertake "further research" into ghostly matters, and he would apply himself to studying old volumes or to reading the latest reports and the news of fresh sightings of ghosts.

Mrs. Scant would have been at her own desk for half an hour by then, sorting out the mail—assuming it had already arrived and, if not, she would wait impatiently for it—or rereading one of her bodice-rippers (as her romantic novels were popularly known).

Old Mr. Copperstone, meanwhile, might hang a notice on the outer handle of his door, informing his staff that he was not to be disturbed as an important meeting was underway.

But they all knew this meant that he was having forty winks in his leather armchair and just conferring with himself.

So all in all, there was little to do at the Ministry of Ghosts except try to look busy—which was quite an exhausting business in itself. Few things are more tiring than having little to do while being compelled to appear as though that little is a lot.

There were crosswords to be discreetly done, of course. There were letters to newspapers to be written on the pertinent affairs of the day. Miss Rolly regularly fired them off to the dailies, giving them the views of the liberated woman. She was always forthright in her expression of those views and seldom held back. But the letters rarely made it as far as the newspaper editors. For the letters were first passed on to Mrs. Scant . . .

"When you have a free moment, Mrs. Scant, if you could type these up. Though obviously Ministry business must take priority . . ."

Yet, even when there was no Ministry business that day, the letters somehow never got dealt with. They remained in Mrs. Scant's inbox until the pile grew so large that they had to be transferred to Mrs. Scant's garbage can, and from there to Mrs. Scant's shredding machine—an old, non-electrical, mechanical contraption operated by a winding handle.

But Miss Rolly seemed unperturbed by this. She did not appear to wonder why her letters never showed up in the newspapers. Maybe she thought that the editors found them too radical to publish. So she went on writing them, more than anything else because it gave her something to do.

Every afternoon, when the minute hand was at the ten and the hour hand at the two, old Mr. Copperstone would summon his staff to his office for a report on how things were going and on general work in progress.

"And so," he would say. "What news, Miss Rolly? Anything conclusive yet?"

Miss Rolly would point at her assistant, Mr. Gibbings, and say, "I delegated matters to Mr. Gibbings, Mr. Copperstone. I am sure that he will be able to give you a full report of our work and activities to date."

The eyes of his superiors would peer expectantly at Mr. Gibbings, who would clear his throat and smooth his thinning hair—for though he was still a young man, he was no longer as young as he once had been at the very start of being young—and he would indicate Mrs. Scant and say, "Mrs. Scant has been kind enough to rustle up my report for me, which I dictated to her earlier. Mrs. Scant, if you would be so kind . . ."

And Mrs. Scant would read from a sheet of typing paper and invariably recount as follows:

"Investigations are continuing into all credible reports of apparitions, ghostly manifestations, and visitors into the material universe from the world of spirit. As yet no conclusive proof has been produced as to the existence of so-called 'ghosts.' The search, therefore, goes on in a diligent and timely manner, and it is hoped that the Ministry will soon have sufficient evidence and material at its disposal to compile a thorough and conclusive report. Meanwhile, no lead remains uninvestigated and no stone unturned. The Ministry of Ghosts continues to maintain its customary high standards and benchmarks."

Mrs. Scant didn't really need to read from the paper, for she knew what to say by heart. She had said the same thing every working day for umpteen years.

She also knew that as soon as she had said her piece, Mr. Copperstone would thank her; he would nod with satisfaction; he would verbally express it; he would indicate his desire that the good work should continue; then he would dismiss his staff. Once they had gone, he would hang his IMPORTANT MEETING UNDERWAY—DO NOT DISTURB sign on his door handle—and soon the sound of deep snoring would resonate through the premises.

So, all in all, the atmosphere and ambience in the Ministry of Ghosts was of a sepia-tinted hue. Life and time moved at the speed and rhythm of the slow-ticking, pendulum-driven grandfather clock in the hallway. A tick, a long pause, and then a tock. Another tick, another long pause, a tock again. While in a window corner a spider built a web and in a basement room a cat purred.

Sometimes a letter fell through the door; sometimes the telephone was heard to ring. But mostly there was congenial silence, broken only by the sound of friendly conversation, as Miss Rolly entered Mr. Gibbings's office on some pretext in order to chat with him and to give him the benefit of her opinions on the affairs of the world outside. Or Mr. Gibbings might call upon Miss Rolly, needing her advice on some civil service technicality of procedure or precedent—expertise that she would willingly share.

Or Mrs. Scant might make an appearance and ask, "Anyone want tea?" Usually getting the affirmative in reply, she would go off to make it, though it did seem to take her an interminable time to do so. Mrs. Scant had to be the slowest boiler of kettles and warmer of teapots in the world.

Then, ultimately, the snoring upstairs would stop. Old Mr. Copperstone would emerge to remove the sign from the door handle, and he would give every appearance of vitality and of being a man concerned in important affairs. He would summon Miss Rolly, so as to confer with her. He would ask Mrs. Scant to step up, as he had several important letters to dictate. Or perhaps he might require young Mr. Gibbings to attend him, so that they could informally discuss sporting matters and which horse was looking good for the 4:15 at Ascot.

For Mr. Copperstone was, in his way, devilish fond of the young fella, who much reminded him of himself in his own younger days. So Mr. Copperstone would invite young Mr. Gibbings to take a seat, and he would regale him with tales from his early days in the civil service—of those past but exciting times at the Department of Work and Pensions, of the heady days at the Ministry of Agriculture. And young Mr. Gibbings would listen spellbound, feeling—as he heard these stories—just a little inadequate and wondering if he would ever experience the thrill of such swashbuckling clerical adventures for himself.

At length, Mr. Gibbings would be dismissed and would return to his office to put the finishing touches on the work of the day. Then, at last, five thirty would come into view, like an old, slow sailing ship, long awaited and looked for, finally lumbering over the horizon.

"Goodnight, Miss Rolly!"

"Goodnight, Mr. Gibbings!"

"Mrs. Scant!"

"Mr. Gibbings, Miss Rolly!"

"Goodnight!"

They would all call goodnight to their revered superior, who would wave to them from the top of the stairs—for old Mr. Copperstone, like the captain of a great liner, knew where his duty lay and made a point of always being the last to leave his ship, sinking or not.

Soon all was silence, save for the ticking of the clock and the mewing of the cat. The motes of dust seemed frozen in the air, as if to be held there for all eternity. Outside, the sky darkened and night came, and some said that as the chimes of midnight rang, then ghosts would walk the earth. But if that were so, then it had never been satisfactorily demonstrated to the standards of proof required at the Ministry of Ghosts.

And so things might have gone on indefinitely. Had it not been for an unexpected caller—one with economies on his mind, a man looking to make big cuts in government expenditures.

Yes, Mr. Franklin Beeston—somewhat like the Grim Reaper, only with a briefcase in his hand instead of a scythe—was on his way to the Ministry of Ghosts to cut down the superfluous corn and to trim the parasitic weeds.

4
AN INSPECTOR CALLS

Mr. Beeston could have driven, but that would have been an extra expense for the government, so he took the bus, and then walked.

"Would you like me to call the Ministry and announce your arrival, Mr. Beeston?" Mrs. Peeve had inquired before he left.

"Of course I don't," he reminded her—having explained this already. "What's the good of a surprise inspection when there's no surprise in it?"

"Oh yes," Mrs. Peeve said. "I don't suppose a surprise inspection would be very useful if they knew you were coming."

"I'd be very surprised if it was, Mrs. Peeve. If you give people advance notice of surprise inspections, then they start to tidy everything up before you get there, and they try to look busy." Mr. Beeston put on his coat. "No, if I gave them any warning at that Ministry of Ghosts, they'd be up to all sorts of tricks, trying to justify their existence. They'd be off to the joke shop buying up fluorescent skeletons and skulls that glow in the dark and bottles of trick bat's blood and what have you. Or hiring a ventriloquist. And they'd no doubt be rigging up hidden apparatus to make it seem like spooks were in the place, all moaning and groaning and making funny smells."

"Funny smells, Mr. Beeston?"

"Visitors from the spirit world are allegedly well known for leaving funny smells behind them."

"Really? And not just visitors from the spirit world, I'd say."

"Well, we won't speak of that for now. But I'll be on to them, don't you worry, Mrs. Peeve. They'll have a hard job pulling the wool over my eyes, and if they do try to, I'll see through it in an instant."

"Oh, you can see through wool then, can you, Mr. Beeston?"

"It's a trick I learned in the army."

"Oh, were you in the army then?"

"I must have been, Mrs. Peeve, or I could hardly have learned tricks there."

"I didn't know they did tricks in the army. I always thought it was more fighting."

"We're getting off the point, Mrs. Peeve, which is that on no account is anyone at the Ministry of Ghosts to be tipped off about this inspection."

"I won't tell them, sir. In fact, I don't even know if I could if I wanted to."

"Oh?"

"Well, thinking you might need it, Mr. Beeston, I tried to find their phone number for you, in the internal directory, but it doesn't seem to be listed."

"Oh?"

"So, I tried to get their email address then, but I couldn't find that, either. But I'll look again."

"They're plainly lying low and trying to keep an inconspicuous profile, Mrs. Peeve, in the hope that they'll never be noticed and that they can go on idling their time away on this well-paid, cushy little number forever. That's what they're up to. They make sure they're on the payroll though, don't they?"

"I assume so. I can't see civil servants working for nothing."

"But I'm going to go over there this morning, Mrs. Peeve, and I'm going to say to them—'Justify this department's existence. Demonstrate your usefulness. Show me what you've been doing here for the last umpteen years. In other words—show me the ghosts!'"

"Show you the ghosts? You think they'll be able to do that, Mr. Beeston?"

"No, Mrs. Peeve, I do not. I think that the Ministry of Ghosts is a redundant relic from another age that should have been done away with years ago. I'm going to put it to them straight. The proof of the pudding is in the eating, and the proof of the ghosts is in the . . . well . . . the seeing. So, I shall want to see them."

"But what if they *have* found some ghosts, Mr. Beeston, only they're invisible? I mean, what if they've got the ghost of the Invisible Man around there, or someone like that?"

"Then I shall demand to see him, too! And if they can't produce him, there'll be hell to pay! Heads will roll, Mrs. Peeve! If I find out that these four civil servants at the Ministry of Ghosts have been idling their time away at the taxpayers' cost, thinking they have been forgotten about and that they can go on in that way indefinitely, well, I shall have a shock ready. I shall fire all of them!"

"Can you do that, Mr. Beeston? Don't you have to go through the proper channels first?"

Mr. Beeston looked rather aggrieved and disappointed, but he had to acknowledge the truth of Mrs. Peeve's observation.

"Unfortunately you're right," he said. "But if I can't get them fired, then I shall have them redeployed to somewhere wet, cold, and windy, where they'll hate every moment of it."

"What, like the Bahamas, you mean?" Mrs. Peeve said.

Mr. Beeston gave her a doubtful look and said, "No, Mrs. Peeve. Not the Bahamas. What I had in mind was the Ministry of Sewage."

Mr. Beeston buttoned up his coat, took his briefcase (containing his lunch), and said, "Hold down the fort, Mrs. Peeve. I may be back soon. I may be back late. But I shall be back."

"Right you are, sir. Best of luck."

"Luck doesn't enter into it," Mr. Beeston said. "It's hard work and diligence that make the difference. Luck is but a spectator, looking on."

"Okey-dokey, sir," Mrs. Peeve said.

Mr. Beeston gave her a withering look. He'd need to talk to her about her language at some point. Okey-dokey was not an approved civil service expression. He just hoped she didn't say it on the phone to callers. If she ever said okey-dokey to someone calling from the House of Lords, there'd be red faces all around. And complaints to go with them.

Mr. Beeston left the departmental building and went to catch his bus. It turned out to be a double-decker and he sat on the upper part, gazing out of the window, his briefcase on his lap, his arms folded upon it. The bus journey took a good half hour or more, and it carried Mr. Beeston into unfamiliar parts of the city, passing places he had not seen or ventured into since he was a boy. Some passengers disembarked along the route and a few new ones got on. But, ultimately, Mr. Beeston was the sole traveler, being taken deep into the old—even ancient—part of town. The skyscrapers and the tall office buildings of shiny glass had long since been left behind on the other side of the river. Here it was Tudor beams and Georgian facades, mews and narrow alleyways leading to dead ends or to even narrower lanes and hidden passageways.

The bus came to a halt and the driver's voice called, "End of the line! Five-minute stop then back again!"

Mr. Beeston got to his feet and hobbled down the stairs—for one of his legs had gone to sleep and was having trouble waking up.

The bus driver heard Mr. Beeston's step. "You the last one, sir?"

"I am," he confirmed. "I wonder if you might be able to direct me to Bric-a-Brac Street."

"Bric-a-Brac? Now, let me see . . . You're sure it's not Nick-Nack Street you're after?"

"No, it isn't."

"Or Tic-Tac Street?"

"No."

"Or Hiccup Road?"

"No, I have the address written down right here. The Ministry of Ghosts, twenty-one Bric-a-Brac Street."

"The Ministry of . . . ?"

"Yes. Ghosts. You did hear correctly."

"Well, hmm . . . won't the street be in your *A to Z* there?"

"Yes, it is, only it's terribly small print and hard to read and rather difficult to follow."

"Well, I'm not a hundred percent, sir, but I think your best bet would be straight on ahead down Codger Row, left at the end, then right, then you'll be in Jumble Crescent, and I'd guess that Bric-a-Brac Street will run off there. It's the old junk and secondhand furniture area, you see, around there. Or at least it was, once upon a time. Hence the street names."

"Right. Well, thank you for your help."

"You're welcome, sir. Buses back on the hour, every hour, until eight o'clock."

"And that's the last one?"

"It is, sir."

"Doesn't the bus service finish rather early?"

"No demand, sir. The buses were just running empty after that time, so the company stopped them. Nobody comes down here in the evening."

"But don't people live here?"

"A few. Mostly just little shops and family businesses here now. A few residential units but not all that many.

Though there is a school. I guess people here just don't stay out late or they have their own transport."

"How odd," Mr. Beeston said, and just as he did, a man on a bicycle shot past. But it wasn't a cyclist in bright-yellow Lycra and padded shorts and white helmet. It was someone in tweeds and a flat cap, and the bike he was riding had one enormous front wheel and one very tiny back one. The front wheel was so big and the seat of the bicycle so high up from the ground that it seemed the only way to get down from the bike was to take a leap and risk significant injury.

"Good lord," Mr. Beeston said. "A penny farthing!"

"He's a maniac, him," the bus driver said. "Seen him before. Rides that bike like he's on a suicide mission."

"Right, well, I'll be getting along."

"Just ask a local if you get lost," the helpful bus driver said.

Only, once the cyclist had gone by, there appeared to be no other locals—not visible ones. They had to be at their jobs, hard at work behind closed doors.

"Does seem odd though," Mr. Beeston again conjectured as he stepped down from the bus platform, "that nobody comes here at night."

"Maybe they're afraid of the ghosts, huh?" the driver joked.

Mr. Beeston gave him a serious and professional look.

"I know it may come as a disappointment to some," Mr. Beeston said, "but there are no such things as ghosts. In fact, it is ghosts that have brought me here. Or rather the lack of them. And I am about to see to it that the futile pursuit of these mythical items is soon to come to a very sudden and abrupt halt!"

"Oh," the bus driver said. "I always thought of ghosts as just a bit of fun, myself."

"Fun?" Mr. Beeston said. "I'm in the civil service. Fun has got nothing to do with it."

So, on he went, briefcase in one hand, his *A to Z* map in the other. He walked on down Codger Row, and then took a left, as instructed. Soon he was in a maze of cobbled streets, where old signs swung overhead in the light morning breeze, speaking of old trades and ancient surnames and of skills in decline or even long gone and quite extinct.

He got lost and then found his bearings again, and then he spotted the brewer's carriage trundling along behind the carthorse, and he felt more confident and more certain that he was on the right road.

Then there it was, the street name he searched for—there on the corner, the turning into Bric-a-Brac Street. The signpost was flaking, its lettering peeling away, but the name was still visible. The cobblestones of the street were worn and uneven. You could almost hear the horses and the trundling carts and the hansom cabs of yesteryear rattling over them. You could all but hear the calls of the dairymaids who had brought their milk to sell in town: "Who will buy, who will buy?" You could smell the past, the scent of fresh flowers brought into the markets, the apples, the bunches of herbs, of rosemary and sage and the perfume of lavender for a lady's room or a gentleman's buttonhole. All gone, and yet still there, impregnated into the fabric of the scenery.

Mr. Beeston stepped gingerly along, not quite at his ease, yet not really knowing why. Then he told himself that he was a professional man with a job to do and not prone to hysteria and fanciful notions.

He heard and then saw the man on the penny farthing again, who juddered so severely over the cobbles on his big-and-little-wheeled bike that he nearly lost his cap.

"Good morning," Mr. Beeston called.

But the man seemed not to hear him and did not reply. Then Mr. Beeston was there, right outside the building, and there was its tarnished brass nameplate. (Very tarnished, he was displeased to note. Couldn't they have done a bit of polishing?)

The Ministry of Ghosts, the lettering told him. And, somewhat unexpectedly and incongruously beneath that, further lettering read: VISITORS BY APPOINTMENT ONLY.

Mr. Beeston gave one of his out loud snorts—even though there was no one there to appreciate it. By appointment, indeed! Did they expect to find ghosts that way? By making appointments with them? What a mess. What a disgrace. And look at the cobwebs in those windows. They should be ashamed to call themselves civil servants. Cobwebs! What were they thinking?

Beneath the words VISITORS BY APPOINTMENT ONLY was one further piece of instruction. This said: DELIVERIES—PLEASE RING BELL.

But Mr. Beeston was not a man for the pathetic ringing of tinkling bells. Oh no. Mr. Beeston was a man who came with thunder and who left with lightning and who announced himself with force and drama. He wanted it to be understood from the start that here was someone to be reckoned with.

So no namby-pamby, itsy-bitsy bells for him.

Mr. Beeston reached up with his free hand, and he took hold of the moldy yet still magnificent knocker on the door, and despite the rust that tried unsuccessfully to restrain his efforts, he beat upon the door with the knocker to such effect that the dust flew and the windows trembled and the very cobblestones seemed to shake in fear.

The noise echoed through the building like an explosion. Old Mr. Copperstone stirred from his slumbers. Mrs. Scant looked up from her desk. Miss Rolly glanced up from a pamphlet she was reading on the rights of women. And Mr. Gibbings looked up from the newspaper crossword puzzle, which he had been attempting to solve for quite some time.

What, each of them wondered, *was that?*

Maybe it was nothing serious, merely an engine backfiring. If they just ignored it . . . Yes, best to just ignore it. Ignore life's little unpleasantnesses and they will usually just go away.

Boom, boom, boom!

There it was again. The same terrible noise followed by the same appalling silence—silence that betokened unexpected callers, that threatened visitors, that spoke of change to an ancient and established way of living.

Boom, boom, boom, boom! Thud! Boom!

What was the *thud*? How the *thud*? Never a *thud* before. Old Mr. Copperstone had never heard a *thud*. Not in all the days of his Ministry. Oh yes, there had been deliveries, there had been callers, there had been the ringing of the doorbell and the occasional *boom* of the knocker. But never a *thud* to go with them. How had it been accomplished? Whoever had managed such a thing? Not just a *boom*, but a *thud*.

Mr. Copperstone crept from his office and out onto the stairs. His staff was already there assembled, looking up to him for guidance and counsel.

"Mr. Copperstone, sir," young Mr. Gibbings said. "There appears to be someone—" But he could not finish the sentence, so overtaken was he by emotion.

"At the door," Miss Rolly said, taking over. "We seem to have—"

"A caller," Mrs. Scant said.

Poor old Mr. Copperstone just stared at them in bewilderment, as though his years of leadership were behind him and his talents had turned to rust through long disuse.

"A caller?" he said. "But we've not had a caller in . . . in years. I wonder . . . what do they want? Who could it be?"

Boom, boom, boom, boom! Then once more that mysterious and terrifying *thud*!

"Perhaps if we just all stand still and keep quiet—"
Boom, boom, boom! Crash!

A *crash* now as well. The caller could do *crashes*, too.

"I don't think they're going to go away, Mr. Copperstone, sir," young Mr. Gibbings observed. And rightly so. For the caller was not about to go anywhere other than inside the building presently closed to him.

"I know you're in there!"

"He knows we're in here," Mr. Copperstone repeated in a whisper. "What are we to do?"

"I think we'll have to let him in, sir," Miss Rolly said.

"It's Head Office here!" the caller shouted from the other side of the door. "Department of Economies!"

"It's Head Office!" Mr. Copperstone repeated. And he might have added the words "we're doomed." But the expression on his face and the look in his eyes said it all, really.

"Let's just sit tight, and he'll go away. They've gone away before," Mrs. Scant said. "Haven't they, over the years? They've gone away before, and so they'll go away again. Stands to reason. Just got to wait them out."

Boom, boom, boom! Thud! Crash! Jingle jangle!

"Oh, my. Good lord!" Mr. Copperstone said. "He can do jingle jangles as well. We've never had a *boom*, a *crash*, a *thud*, and a *jingle jangle* before, ever."

"I'm afraid he means business," Miss Rolly said. "We're going to have to let him in or by the sound of it, he'll break the door down."

"Let me in, or I have an authorization document here signed by the Executive Admin. Department, entitling me to break the door down. And the subsequent repairs and new door lock will have to come out of your budget!"

"Our budget," Mr. Copperstone said. "That's rather unfair. I don't see why we have to pay for his breaking the door down. I shall be writing a few strongly worded letters to the Cabinet Office if that—"

"I think, sir, we'd better let him in, don't you?"

"I'm afraid, Mr. Gibbings, that you might be right. Are we all agreed?" They nodded. "Shall we go together then? All for one and one for all as it were?"

So, shoulder to shoulder, they went to the front door, and the lock was turned and the security bolt slid back. Outside, Mr. Beeston found the handle turning now and the door responding to his grip, finally yielding to the force of his arm and his personality.

The door swung open, accompanied by such a fine collection of creaks that it was almost a symphony. There was Mr. Beeston on the doorstep. And there were Mr. Copperstone, Miss Rolly, Mr. Gibbings, and Mrs. Scant ready to greet him. But no warm words were said. There were no endearing or flavorsome greetings.

"Head Office," Mr. Beeston said. "My ID, if you'd care to see it. I'm here to do an inspection. I've got a list of staff here. I assume that you will be Mr. Copperstone?"

"At your service," Mr. Copperstone said, putting on his bravest face and his most suave manner. But he felt neither suave nor brave within. He invited Mr. Beeston to step inside with the utmost trepidation.

Down in the basement, even Boddington the cat, hitherto silent, seemed to cower in dread anticipation.

5

A DIFFICULT INTERVIEW

Tea, sir?" Mrs. Scant asked. "Tea, Mr. . . . ?"

"Beeston," Beeston said. "Franklin Beeston. And no, thank you. I am not here to drink tea. I am here on more compelling matters."

"Tea for you then, Mr. Copperstone?"

"Um, thank you, Mrs. Scant, that would be rather . . ."

Mr. Copperstone caught sight of the solemn and sour expression of the man sitting in the visitor's chair on the opposite side of his desk, and he changed his mind. Tea suddenly seemed rather frivolous, not a thing to be bothering with right then.

"Um, not just now, thank you all the same, Mrs. Scant. Maybe later."

"Very well, sir. And will you be wanting me here to take any dictation?"

Beeston's look said no, that the meeting was to be a confidential one.

"No, thank you, Mrs. Scant. I'll call if anything's needed."

"Very well, sir."

"And close the door after you, please," Mr. Beeston commanded. Mrs. Scant didn't care for his tone nor the implication that she was one to eavesdrop or to snoop.

She made her way to the door with all the dignity she could muster, let it close behind her, walked away down the hall, stopped, tiptoed silently back, then applied her ear and her eye to the keyhole—these items taking regular turns.

"So, what can I do for you here today, Mr. . . . um . . . Beeston? To what do we owe this unexpected visit and undeserved honor?"

"I wouldn't bank on the 'honor,' Mr. Copperstone. Not a bit."

"Oh . . . ?"

In truth, Mr. Copperstone felt nervous. Although the senior man, both in years and in rank, he felt now as he had when a small boy and suddenly summoned before the principal for he knew not what. But he always soon found out. And rarely liked it.

"The fact is, Mr. Copperstone, that I am, as I said, from the Department of Economies—"

"You did, and yet I didn't even realize there was such a department."

"There is, Mr. Copperstone. There has been for some years. And one by one we have been auditing all the other departments. And a few weeks ago, down the back of the filing cabinet, I found you."

"Me? That is, us? Behind a filing cabinet?"

"All your departmental information. I have it here. Such as it is." Mr. Beeston extracted a Manila folder from his briefcase.

"Oh yes?" Mr. Copperstone said, appearing to look both interested and unperturbed.

"I—nor anyone else, it seemed—even knew of the existence of this place. We were astonished to learn of it. It seemed incomprehensible that there should be such a department in the modern world—"

"Well, we strive to do good work here . . ."

"I shall be coming to that."

"Oh."

"Founded seventeen ninety-two, I understand?"

"I believe it to be the case."

"In order to prove or to disprove the existence of spiritual manifestations colloquially known as 'ghosts.'"

"Indeed, that is our function. The Ministry is a venerable institution."

"It's that or a useless one. Because this institution has now been in operation for well over two centuries. It has absorbed huge amounts of taxpayers' money. And what, Mr. Copperstone, has this department discovered after two hundred years of investigation? Do ghosts exist or don't they?"

Mr. Copperstone took a moment to answer. Mr. Beeston pressed him to reply.

"Yes or no, sir?"

But it was not, Mr. Copperstone felt, a yes or no question with a no or a yes answer. It was more complex than that.

"Well?"

"Results to date have been somewhat inconclusive," Mr. Copperstone said. "But rest assured that investigations are continuing, and we hope to have some answers soon."

Mr. Beeston put the Manila folder down on the desk.

"No, sir," he said. "I am afraid not. I am here to inform you that investigations are not continuing."

"Not . . . ?" A look of concern crossed Mr. Copperstone's face; he reached for his breast pocket, as if troubled by his heart.

"If this department has been unable, after more than two hundred years of looking, to discover whether ghosts exist, then there is only one possible conclusion to be drawn. Don't you think?"

"That the ghosts are hiding?" Mr. Copperstone suggested.

"No!" Mr. Beeston snapped. "That there aren't any, of course. There are no such things. And it is a complete waste of time and money to go on looking for them. How many of you work here? I have it down as four. Correct?"

"Four plus the cat," Mr. Copperstone said.

"Oh yes, the cat. And what's he doing? Idling on the job, is he?"

"I expect he'll be in the basement, keeping the mice at bay."

"Maybe he's keeping the ghosts at bay, too, and that's why you never catch any."

"You know, I've never considered that. Do you think that could be it? That ghosts and cats are allergic to each other?"

"I was not being serious. That was sarcasm."

"Oh, sarcasm. Oh."

"The fact is, Mr. Copperstone, that this department is in serious trouble. To be blunt, the government deems your Ministry to be a product of the dark ages of myth and superstition, and one that cannot be tolerated in the modern world. In short, the present government does not believe that so-called 'ghosts' exist, and if you cannot prove otherwise then the Department of Paranormal Affairs—aka the Ministry of Ghosts—will be shut down permanently. Unless you can very rapidly justify your existence, it will be closed forever."

"Closed down! But—good heavens—all our exemplary work here . . ."

Mr. Beeston folded his arms and sat back in his chair. "Oh yes. Your exemplary work. Tell me a little about that if you would, Mr. Copperstone. How exactly do you and your staff go about determining the existence of ghosts? What precisely do you do all day?"

"Do?"

"Yes, do?"

"Well . . ."

"Do you go out and scour the locality for ghosts? Do you go off on ghost-hunting expeditions? Do you travel the world to investigate reported sightings? Do you run down to the cemetery in the evening . . . ?"

"Well, not in the evening, no, as that would mean overtime . . ."

"During the day, then? Or what?"

"No, I think you misunderstand the nature of our work here, Mr. Beeston. What we try to do here, you see, is not so much to go out in search of ghosts as to try to create contact with the spirit world. To get the ghosts to come to us."

"And how do you do that?"

44

"We ask the relevant and appropriate questions, sir."

"Such as?"

"Well, we say things like, 'Is anyone there?'"

"Is anyone there?"

"Or, 'Who's that?'"

"Who's that?"

"Or, 'Give us a sign!'"

"A sign?"

"Or we have the occasional séance together and try to get the ghosts to spell things out on our Ouija board. Which reminds me, I was going to put in a request to buy a new Ouija board, as ours seems to be wearing out."

"And has anyone ever made contact from the spirit world via your civil service–issued Ouija board?"

"Not what you might call contact as such. But we keep on trying. Every Tuesday."

"Mr. Copperstone!"

"Mr. Beeston?"

The two men were so different in character they were almost of separate species. One was old school; one was new. Copperstone was all old-world charm and half-moon glasses, over which he could peer in a most engaging way. He was a man who was exceedingly well-read and who could converse on any subject under the sun. He could tell you about his school days and his time in India; about his childhood with his friend Chubby Smitterton and the incident with the sausages. He could regale you with anecdotes until the cows came home, got milked, and wandered away again.

But Mr. Copperstone's anecdotes were wasted on Mr. Beeston, who was all about "time" and "efficiency" and "value for money." Mr. Copperstone, with his elegant, inlaid cufflinks and his handmade shoes, was a mystery to him. No, modern times had suddenly entered the offices of the Ministry of Ghosts and like it or not, Mr. Copperstone and his staff were to be dragged into them, if necessary by the scruffs of their necks.

"Mr. Copperstone, tell me this—what do you and your staff do all day? Describe an average day to me. Tell me about it."

"Well, let me see . . ."

Under the elegant exterior, panic was rising. Mr. Copperstone—when faced with the question as to what he did all day—wasn't sure that he knew the answer. He knew he did the crossword; he knew he had forty winks; he knew he later on had another forty winks—making eighty winks in total, but surely other people had more. It wasn't that much, was it? Not eighty winks. Not when you considered all the winks you could have if you put your mind to it.

"Well, we, I . . . that is . . . we come in, we open the mail, if there is any—"

"And is there?"

"We do get quite a few flyers for pizza—"

"So, you come in and deal with the mail. That sounds as if it takes you all of five minutes. Then what?"

"Then my secretary, Mrs. Scant, will ask if we want some tea—"

"Tea!"

"Then, after that, we'll get down to the hard graft."

"That's the bit I'm interested in. Tell me more about that."

"That's when we get down to trying to make contact with the spirit world by using all the means at our disposal."

"Such as the Ouija board?"

"Yes."

"And calling out, 'Is anybody there?'"

"Yes, but you have to keep doing it," Mr. Copperstone explained. "It's no use just calling the once and expecting an immediate answer."

"What else do you do?" Mr. Beeston demanded.

"Well, we . . . we might put a little notice in the window."

"Saying what?"

"Um, well, saying: GHOST WANTED, NO EXPERIENCE NECESSARY. Or, GHOST WANTED. SMALL REWARD GIVEN. Or—"

"And so far, what have all these efforts produced?"

"Well, as I say, things are still rather up in the air. But rest assured, Mr. Beeston, we are ever vigilant. And one day soon we hope to be able to announce to the world that ghosts either do or do not exist. And that will be our finest hour."

Mr. Beeston had now come to the end of his rope. He snatched the file from the desk and stuffed it back into his briefcase, next to his thermos and sandwiches.

"Mr. Copperstone—shall I tell you what I think?"

"Please do. I'm always keen to hear the opinions of others."

"Mr. Copperstone, I have worked for the Department of Economies for some time. Prior to that, I worked for the Ministry of Social Security investigating bogus claims. I pride myself on being able to smell a rat."

"They can smell bad," Mr. Copperstone agreed. "Especially the dead ones. Fortunately for us, we have the cat."

"I have never, in the course of all my investigations, come across a more pointless, useless, time-and-money-wasting department than this one."

Mr. Copperstone blinked at him, uncertain of what he was hearing. There was some mistake, surely. This man couldn't be serious.

"I am giving you, Mr. Copperstone, precisely three months in which to prove the need for a Ministry of Ghosts. Three calendar months from today to come up with a so-called ghost. If, by the end of that time, you have failed to produce one, then I am going to recommend to the Minister that this department be closed down."

"C-close us down?"

"Immediately, on expiration of the deadline. And permanently."

"C-close down the Ministry of Ghosts? B-but, it has been in existence since—"

"I know!"

"Seventeen ninety-two."

"It doesn't matter how long it has been in existence; it is now looking very redundant. It has outlived whatever usefulness it once had and I doubt it ever had any. It seems to me that it is about as relevant to the modern world as the Department of Horse-Drawn Vehicles—which is now defunct."

"Did we have one of those?"

"Or the Ministry of Witchcraft."

"I didn't realize—"

"Or the Department of Rubbing Sticks Together to Start a Fire—"

"Did we really—"

"No, of course not. I just say it to illustrate how out of date your department is. You have three months, Mr. Copperstone, to produce a ghost. And not just some fake ghoul from the joke shop. A real live—well, dead, actually, I suppose—ghost. If you can't do it, then we must conclude, after more than two hundred years of searching, that ghosts don't exist. So the need for your department will be no more."

"But what's to become of us?" Mr. Copperstone said, very alarmed by now. "Myself, my staff, who have given such loyal service—"

"I dare say they'll be redeployed somewhere. I hear that the Ministry of Sewage has some vacancies that need to be filled."

"Sewage? The Sewage Department? My staff?"

"While, as for yourself, sir, it would seem to me—and no rudeness intended—that retirement might well be an option."

Mr. Copperstone looked shocked, even bereft. "Retire? Me? Retire? But—"

"You seem of an age, sir, if you don't mind my saying . . ."

"Yes, but what would I do all day?"

"The same as you do now, by the looks of it, sir—not much!"

"Now, see here . . ." Old Mr. Copperstone was on his feet. He was an easygoing man but Mr. Beeston had gone too far.

"*You* see here," Mr. Beeston said. "Three months. From today. Soon as I get back to my office, I shall put it in writing and mail it to you. I'll also send you an email."

Mr. Copperstone looked blank. "Email?"

Mr. Beeston stared around the room. "Where are your computers?"

"Computers?" Mr. Copperstone said. "Are you speaking of that Babbage fellow? Isn't he trying to build one?"

"For heaven's sake!" Mr. Beeston said. "How behind the times are you here? Haven't you kept up with modern developments?"

"Of course we have. We have the telephone."

Mr. Copperstone pointed to the rather antique-looking instrument on his desk.

"Yes, you'll need to give me the number for that. It's not in our files. And you'd better get yourself an Apple or a PC."

"An apple? I don't eat them. It's my teeth—"

"An Apple with a capital A! Or a PC!"

"PC Apple? Police Constable Apple? Who's he?"

"I give up," Mr. Beeston said. "What on earth have you been doing here? Do you even so much as stick your noses out of the door?"

"One does not have to travel in order to seek out the spirit world," Mr. Copperstone said. "For the spirit world—if it is here—must be all around us. It's not a matter of traveling to the four corners of the earth; it's a matter of finding a way through, of finding the key."

"Well, this department has had over two hundred years to look for it and the key hasn't turned up. So, I don't think there is a key. Or a door. Or anything. I think this whole place is pointless."

"Pointless! The venerable Ministry of Ghosts?"

"As you so plainly think otherwise, you have three months in which to prove me wrong. I shall be back in precisely three months' time. You've had it far too easy for far too long. The taxpayers won't put up with it any longer!"

"I don't think the taxpayers even know we're—"

"They will when I tell them. And they'll be outraged. Outraged! Don't bother seeing me to the door, I shall find my own way out. Good day to you, sir."

"Good day to you, my dear fellow. Allow me to . . ."

The good manners ingrained in Mr. Copperstone compelled him to see his visitor out. In the hall, hearing their approach, Mrs. Scant scuttled away before the door could be opened and her eavesdropping revealed.

She hurried down the stairs to her office, where she sat in front of her typewriter, looking pale and shocked. Soon she heard voices and the sound of Mr. Beeston leaving and of Mr. Copperstone bidding him farewell.

"Three months, remember. From today."

Those were Mr. Beeston's parting words as the door creaked shut behind him, then all that could be heard were the sounds of his footsteps receding over the cobblestones.

Silence.

Then the voice of old Mr. Copperstone.

"Mrs. Scant, Mr. Gibbings, Miss Rolly—could I ask you all to join me in my office for a moment? I have some rather grave and important news."

They heard him and called back that they were on their way.

Mr. Copperstone returned to his office. His heart was heavy and his eyes were full. He could feel in his elderly bones all the passing of the years, and he wondered if the struggle had—after all—been in vain. Was this what it had come to? To be forcibly retired, after a life of service and dedication? To be thrown in the trash? To be flung aside like some poor, unwanted thing? Like an outgrown toy, cast aside by a thoughtless child?

It was hard not to feel sorry for oneself, and yet self-pity was not really in Mr. Copperstone's nature. He had his staff to think of. He had to put them first. So he pulled himself together, and he wondered how he was going to break the news to them—that they had three months in which to produce a ghost or their department would be closed down permanently.

But Mrs. Scant had already informed the others. They already knew the worst. Even so, they entered the office as if in ignorance. Out of deference to, and respect for, old Mr. Copperstone, they allowed him to break the news to them all over again. And they did their best to appear as though that news were indeed something new.

6

A WAY TO CATCH A GHOST

The sounds of Mr. Franklin Beeston's footsteps echoed through the Ministry of Ghosts long after he had gone.

Old Mr. Copperstone sat behind his mahogany desk, while arranged around the room in front of him, in various attitudes of dejection, his staff waited for him to speak—though they knew already what was to be said.

"That . . . person," Mr. Copperstone began. "That . . . person who has just left was from the Department of Economies. He was here, he said, to trim the dead wood."

"Dead wood?" Miss Rolly interjected. "I hope that isn't how he sees us."

"It's exactly how he sees us, Miss Rolly, I am afraid to say. He is of the opinion that our Ministry here is old-fashioned and redundant and—it pains me to repeat it—he believes that our work here is pointless and unnecessary. He doesn't believe that ghosts exist."

"Not exist? No ghosts?" young Mr. Gibbings said, incredulous. "Then what have we been working here for all these years? And the people who worked here before us?"

"Exactly," Mr. Copperstone said. "All because the Ministry of Ghosts hasn't come up with a ghost in the past two hundred years or so doesn't mean they don't exist. It could just mean that ghosts are very good at hiding and at disguising themselves, and they are somewhat on the sneaky side."

"They could be absolutely everywhere!" Mrs. Scant agreed.

"There could be dozens of them in this room with us right now."

"Hundreds!" Miss Rolly said.

"Millions!" Mr. Gibbings said—but Mr. Copperstone gave him a look as though to convey that millions of ghosts in the room was possibly an exaggeration.

"Just because we can't see them doesn't mean they aren't there. After all, can you see electricity?" Miss Rolly said.

"Or magnetism? But they're there, and we know they are, see them or not."

Mr. Copperstone held up a hand for silence.

"Be that as it may," he continued, "none of it would convince a skeptic such as our recent visitor. The crux of the matter is that we have three months from today in which to produce a ghost. A convincing and undeniable ghost. One that looks, sounds, feels, and smells like a ghost—if they do smell."

"They smell of peppermints, according to Throgmorton's *Book of Ghosts*, sir."

"Thank you, Mr. Gibbings. I am aware of the theories. I have read them all."

"Of course, sir. I only meant . . ." But Mr. Gibbings never did finish saying what he meant, his voice just trailed off.

"And what if we don't produce a ghost in time, to that gentleman's satisfaction, Mr. Copperstone?" Miss Rolly said.

"Then the Ministry will be closed down. And those of us still young enough will be redeployed to the Ministry of Sewage—"

"Ministry of Sewage!" Miss Rolly exclaimed. "I don't like the sound of that."

"Nor the smell of it," Mrs. Scant said.

"As for those elder members of staff, such as myself, we will retire. Sent home—for good."

"But, Mr, Copperstone, sir—you have been at the Ministry of Ghosts for . . . well . . . forever."

"I have given my life to it, Mrs. Scant. It will sadden me to leave. It will sadden me even more to have no successor to whom I can pass on the mantle. It will be as though my whole life's work has been . . . in vain."

There was a long, respectful silence. Miss Rolly broke it with a note of optimism.

"Unless, of course, we can find a ghost, sir."

"Easier said than done, Miss Rolly," Mr. Copperstone sighed. "The Ministry has been looking for the things for over two hundred years now. Our predecessors were dedicated men and women. But for all their looking, they found nothing. They have died, and had they wished, or been able, they could have returned as ghosts themselves and could have given us the full facts of life on 'the other side.' But no. Total silence. Not a sound. Not as much as the ghost of a sound. No ghost and no sound at all."

"Then maybe we haven't been looking in the right places, sir," Mr. Gibbings said, for he was young and headstrong and thought that his ideas were sparkling and original and had not been considered before.

"If you read through the archives, Mr. Gibbings, you will see that the Ministry has looked everywhere," Mr. Copperstone said. "Expeditions have been sent out all over the world. When Scott went to Antarctica, he was asked to keep an eye out for ghosts. When Clive went to India, same thing. When Mallory went up Everest, he, too, was requested to keep his eyes peeled and his wits about him. All to no avail. Plenty of reports of strange noises and odd goings-on, oh yes, but a real live ghost to bring home—"

"Or a real dead one, sir," Miss Rolly said.

"What? Oh yes. Quite so. No, to my knowledge we have explored every avenue."

"Sir," Miss Rolly said, "I do believe there is one approach that the Ministry has never adopted."

Mr. Copperstone glanced at her over his half-moon glasses. Was it possible that she was correct?

"What approach is that, Miss Rolly?"

"If I can first just remind you, sir, of Grimes and Natterly's *Manual of Ghost Hunting*."

"The ghost hunter's bible? We all know it well, from cover to cover. It is the handbook of our profession. Our lodestone and guiding star. What of it, Miss Rolly?"

"Does it not say, sir, that ghosts will often appear only to those who have a kind of sixth sense?"

"It does. And?"

"Or to those of a peculiarly naive and innocent nature—pets and animals, for instance. It says that dogs, for example, can become aware of a ghostly presence long before any human knows of it."

"We did have a dog once, when I first started in the Ministry," Mr. Copperstone reminisced. "Very rare breed. A ghost-sniffer he was. But he never sniffed any out as I remember. The only thing he seemed to be good at sniffing out was your ham sandwiches."

"But it's not just dogs, sir. Grimes and Natterly say there are other creatures that ghosts are drawn to."

"Then they have slipped my mind. Remind me, Miss Rolly, what these exotic creatures are."

"Children!" Miss Rolly said. "Children—according to Grimes and Natterly—have a sensitivity that adults do not. A sensitivity they lose as they grow older. But while still young enough, they can not only see ghosts, but they can even attract them, lure them in, as it were. Draw them near to you, as if children were some kind of . . . bait."

Mr. Copperstone looked concerned. He removed his glasses, polished them on his impeccable handkerchief, and returned them to his nose.

"This is all very true, Miss Rolly," he said. "I am aware of it. But the Ministry long ago ruled that the use of children in the luring of ghosts would be to expose those children to trauma and danger, and would be quite unethical."

"Yes, sir," Miss Rolly said. "But in my experience, children are pretty robust sorts of creatures. I can't see that a few ghosts would frighten most of them. Quite the opposite. Children probably frighten ghosts more than the other way around."

"Children certainly frighten me," Mr. Gibbings said. "I saw a bunch of them in the street the other morning, and they were absolutely terrifying. It's a good job I know some Japanese self-defense."

"And our options are rather limited, Mr. Copperstone, sir," Mrs. Scant—who had been pretty quiet for a while—interjected. "And we don't have a lot of time. Beggars can't be choosers, after all."

"Meaning, Mrs. Scant?"

"Meaning, sir, that we're up the creek without a paddle. And if using a child is going to find a ghost for us and save the Ministry and our jobs, well, then maybe we ought to get one."

"Hmm . . ." Mr. Copperstone sat thinking it over. "I'm still concerned at the ethics of it . . . the possible damage—"

"What's the worst that can happen, sir? That the little buggers will have a small scare? Well, they'll soon get over that. And we can pay them. There's quite a bit of money in petty cash this month."

"Hmm . . . yes . . . I see the value of the proposal, Miss Rolly. Only, does anyone here have any children that they could spare for such a job? My own children . . . well . . . they're nearly as old as I am now. Possibly even older. All grown up and off around the world. I never see them. So that is a problem, isn't it, Miss Rolly? We don't have a child to use as ghost bait—if I may put it like that."

"I'm sure we can get one, sir. There's thousands around the place."

"I can't see their parents agreeing to the proposal."

"They might not need to know . . . immediately."

"And where would we get a suitable child from? After all, they don't grow on trees, do they, Miss Rolly?"

"We just advertise, sir. A notice in the window, to start with. Maybe an ad in the newspaper."

"Then, if that doesn't work, a hot-air balloon with an advertisement on the side!" Mr. Gibbings chipped in.

"I don't think the Ministry could afford that, Mr. Gibbings. And I'm sure such an advertisement would breach several hundred regulations."

"Well, we've nothing to lose, in my opinion, Mr. Copperstone," Miss Rolly said. "I, for one, am confident that the ghosts are there. I've felt on numerous occasions that they were right behind me. Or off to my left. Or they'd just left the room as I came into it. Or they came into it as I went out."

"Me, too, Miss Rolly," Mr. Gibbings said excitedly. "I've felt that way also. Always so near, yet always just out of reach. Elusive is the word. But if you want to catch something, you first have to bait the trap. It's all explained in Grimes and Natterly's *Manual of Ghost Hunting*."

"So, did they ever catch one?" Mrs. Scant asked. "Natterly and Grimes?"

"They died in mysterious circumstances before they could put their theories into practice and their plans into action," Mr. Copperstone said.

"Ah . . . mysterious circumstances, huh?" Mrs. Scant said. "I've heard of them."

Mr. Copperstone had by now come to a decision.

"Very well, Miss Rolly—I think your suggestion is our only option and our only hope. We have to give it a try. We can't let the Ministry be closed down. We can't let two hundred years or more of history be snuffed out, just like that. The Ministry of Ghosts is an institution. Is this feeling unanimous?"

It was.

"Very well. Miss Rolly and Mr. Gibbings, would you put your heads together and come up with a suitable advertisement as soon as possible? Which, subject to my approval, we will immediately put up in the window."

"And what would you like me to do, sir?"

"Ah, Mrs. Scant. I wonder if it would be possible for you to make us all a nice cup of tea?"

"Of course it would, sir. A pleasure. I'll go and do it now."

"And maybe you could look in on the cat on your way, Mrs. Scant. I expect I ought to explain what's going on to him at some point. Not that he'll understand, of course. But he is a sort of member of staff."

"If I see him, I'll mention it, sir."

Off Mrs. Scant went to boil the kettle. But, as ever, her tea-making took an interminably long time. You did start to wonder if your tea was ever going to arrive, or whether you'd still want it when it did.

"Thank you all then," Mr Copperstone said to the others. "Let's press on. We might yet save the Ministry of Ghosts from extinction. I hope we do. Yes, I hope we do."

The meeting was over, and all went about their business—apart from Mr. Copperstone himself, who had no real business other than to delegate business to others. He sat behind his desk, waiting for his tea and thinking of the past and of the heady, glory days of ghost hunting. And, little by little, his eyes grew heavy, and one by one (though he did only have the two of them, so it didn't take long) they closed.

Soon a ghostly sound was heard. But it was only someone snoring.

7

WEEKEND BOY WANTED

It was left to youngish Mr. Gibbings to compose the advertisement. It took him most of the morning. Considering what he came up with, this might seem like an overly extravagant expenditure of effort for a slightly meager achievement.

BOY WANTED—his first draft began. Then he decided to be more specific. WEEKEND BOY WANTED, he rewrote. WEEKEND BOY WANTED, MOSTLY FOR SATURDAYS. LIGHT WORK. GOOD WAGES. EASY HOURS.

He studied the paper in front of him. Was Weekend Boy the right thing? What about a Friday Boy instead? Or a Tuesday Boy? Or a Sunday Boy? No. That wouldn't do. Boys were at school from Monday to Friday, and they might have trouble getting away on a Sunday, due to commitments: soccer games, family activities, homework. Best to keep it as it was.

WEEKEND BOY WANTED. MOSTLY FOR SATURDAYS. Well, that was fair enough. It explained the extent of the commitment. It made things clear that a boy was needed only for Saturdays and that would be all.

LIGHT WORK? Was that all right? Or should Mr. Gibbings be more specific? Should he actually say that ghost hunting was involved? Or would that drive away the more timid candidates? But did he want timid candidates? Oh, leave it as is, he decided. No need to deter potential applicants in advance. Get them in, get them interested, get them signed up and started.

Good wages. Would they be? Mr. Gibbings thought so. Good for a weekend job anyway. You didn't have to pay boys a lot for them to think that they were earning big money. A couple of pounds, a few chocolate bars, and a bottle of soda—that would do for most of them. They'd be happy with that. And maybe an apple. Yes, petty cash could probably run to an apple as well.

Anyway, wages could be negotiable. Perhaps he'd better say as much.

Weekend boy wanted, mostly for Saturdays. Light work. Good wages—negotiable. Easy hours.

Easy hours? Well, that rather depended. It might be tough, luring ghosts in. Hard to say. But easy in the sense of duration. You couldn't expect weekend help to work long hours, there were regulations against it. Same as you couldn't go sending boys down coal mines or stuffing them up chimneys any more.

Mind you, back when the Ministry of Ghosts was established, centuries ago, in 1792, boys up chimneys were a regular, even a daily, occurrence. The chances were that whenever you walked along a street, there would be a few houses with boys in their chimneys, endeavoring to sweep them clean, and getting very dirty in the process.

Child labor laws had come a long way in the past two centuries. Children had to go to school now, for years and years. You couldn't send them off to work in pits and in textile factories starting at the age of ten. No, you couldn't leave school these days until you were almost fifty.

Well, maybe not fifty. But Mr. Gibbings remembered his own school days as having gone on forever. They had gone on so long they seemed to have started all over again before he finally got to the end of them.

EASY HOURS. That was fine. LIGHT WORK. EASY HOURS. GOOD WAGES. Oh, but where to apply to? Well, WITHIN, of course. Just ring the bell or use the knocker— if you were tall enough to reach it and strong enough to whack it against the door.

That would do it then. So he made a few small alterations, and his final version read:

WEEKEND BOY WANTED. FOR SATURDAYS ONLY. LIGHT WORK. GOOD WAGES—NEGOTIABLE. EASY HOURS. APPLY WITHIN.

But what about a uniform? Would there be a uniform? No. No uniform. Protective clothing though, maybe.

PROTECTIVE CLOTHING SUPPLIED IF NEEDED.

That should do it. Just a bit of Scotch tape now. Mrs. Scant would have something. And indeed she did. She wasn't at her desk—she was no doubt making tea or talking to the cat. So Mr. Gibbings helped himself. Then he went to the front room on the ground floor, the dusty window of which faced Bric-a-Brac Street, and he polished one of the panes, and he put up the notice.

WEEKEND BOY WANTED. FOR SATURDAYS ONLY.
LIGHT WORK. GOOD WAGES—NEGOTIABLE.

EASY HOURS. APPLY WITHIN.
PROTECTIVE CLOTHING SUPPLIED IF NEEDED.

Should he mention the apple, he wondered, at the last moment. No. Leave the apple for now. It could be mentioned during the interview. It would come as an added inducement, a sort of bonus, a reward for good work.

So the advertisement went up in the window, and Mr. Gibbings retired to his office, to continue with his other work—such as it was that day. But he was too distracted by thoughts of the closure of the Ministry, and of his possible redeployment to the Sewage Department. He didn't like the thought of sewage at all. Give him ghosts any day. Say what you like about them, at least they didn't smell—or if they did, they didn't smell as bad as sewage.

The remaining hours of the morning and the early part of the afternoon passed quietly.

Mr. Copperstone woke from his slumber; Mrs. Scant appeared, with fresh promises of tea; Miss Rolly read about ghosts in her *Ghost and Ectoplasm Manual* and she composed a few letters to various organizations—such as the Spiritualists' Association and the Clairvoyants' Guild—asking if they had yet acquired conclusive evidence of the existence of ghosts that would bear scientific scrutiny. Mr. Gibbings spent some time thinking of Miss Rolly and of what a fine and able civil servant she was, with many exemplary qualities—though he was also a little wary of her, as she was such a staunch feminist and supporter of equal rights.

Perhaps Mr. Gibbings should have asked Miss Rolly to check through his advertisement before he put it up in the window. She would have pointed out his mistake to him immediately. As things were, he did not even know that he had made one.

He was very soon to find out that he had.

8
EUSTACE SCOOL SCHOOL

Although the neighborhood of which Bric-a-Brac Street was a part had the aura of a place that time had passed by and that the greater world had forgotten, for those who lived there life went on with as much urgency and importance as it did in more dynamic places.

True, it wasn't the hub of life's wheel—more the far end of one of the spokes. But even on the circumference of things, existence goes on, and while those on the rim of life's revolving wheel may not be as fashionable as those at the center, they still spin around, if at a slower rate.

The area around Bric-a-Brac Street was not only home to the obscure professions and the forgotten trades. Codger Row did not just house the elderly in its ancient alms houses. There were families living there, too, in old, terraced dwellings, some spacious, some narrow, some with just two rooms upstairs and another two down.

There was a school at the end of the aptly named Scool Street. This was no misspelling or error at the sign maker's. It was a street named after one Mr. Eustace Scool, who had left money for the establishment of a home for foundlings and orphans. That home was now the premises of the local school, named Eustace School—as it had been felt by the governors that to call it Eustace Scool School would only lead to confusion and spelling mistakes.

The school was not a large one. Indeed, it was one of those schools that would soon find itself closed down if the number of its pupils got smaller. Which would have been a great inconvenience. For the next nearest school was a good bus ride away, whereas at the moment, most pupils could walk there from home.

So there was a reasonable flow of children up and down Bric-a-Brac Street throughout the day—first thing in the morning, and then last thing in the afternoon. They scuffed along, usually in no rush either to arrive at school in time or to get home in any hurry. Many of them stopped on the way to enter premises in Dust Street called Mrs. Hallet's Bon-Bons—Sweets and Toffees by Appointment. By whose appointment it was not said.

Dust Street was not so called because it was particularly dusty—no more so than any other street nearby. But it was here that diamond cutters and polishers once plied their trade. And there would be those who would come to sweep up and to buy the dust from their work. They would take the diamond dust away, and who knows what they did with it, but they put it to some kind of use.

Mrs. Hallet's Bon-Bons shop was a cavern of sweet and sticky things. There was no sign on her door saying ONLY TWO SCHOOL CHILDREN AT A TIME PERMITTED.

It was an open house and the place was always busy at 8:30 in the morning and at 3:45 in the afternoon. The rest of the day was quiet. But that did not matter. That was when she made the toffee and boiled sweets. She made enough money at peak times to keep her going. Of course, if the school ever closed, that would be the end of her. So she hoped it never would.

A dozen children a day, at least, must have walked past the Ministry of Ghosts in both directions, and had done so for years . . . for decades . . . for centuries.

Yet none of them knew it was there.

Which is a curious, even an extraordinary, thing. Because children usually have a deep and abiding interest in ghosts. Ghosts seem to fascinate them and to hold them spellbound. And while the thought of ghosts might frighten children, too, there aren't many children who wouldn't like to see one, if only once, and who'd be willing to risk the terror for the privilege of the experience, and to be able to say that they had seen a ghost with their very own eyes—and that they had lived to tell the tale (assuming they did), and that their hair hadn't gone white overnight nor had they been turned to stone.

But not one of the many children who had gone by the Ministry of Ghosts ever realized what they were passing. The Ministry's tarnished brass plate, covered in verdigris and stained by the weather, was fastened to the front of the building at adult height above their heads. They would not have seen it. Or, if they had, would not have been interested by such a moldy, drab, boring-looking thing.

All those children had just walked on by, thinking their thoughts, wrapped up in their own concerns, chatting with their friends, or counting the coins in their hands and wondering what they might get for them from Mrs. Hallet's Bon-Bons shop. Similarly, they would return the same way in the afternoon, now chewing on their toffees and eating their fudge and sucking on lemon drops, and in other ways giving tooth decay a sporting chance.

To them the Ministry of Ghosts was just another dingy building where adult dreariness no doubt went on, where paper was shuffled and forms were filled in, and where 5:30 was a long time coming. So back and forth the children had gone, to and from Eustace School, until they were old enough to go to Eustace Senior School, and then they had left and most had moved on and ceased to walk past the Ministry of Ghosts at all. Once they were tall enough to read the brass plate, they were no longer there to see it.

Only the mailman had an active knowledge of the Ministry of Ghosts, but even he had his doubts about it. Few letters arrived there, and the mailman believed those that did were misaddressed (and that the envelopes should have read "Ministry of Gas").

Or a new mailman would come along and he would think the Ministry of Ghosts to be some kind of a made-up name for a company that sold fancy outfits or novelties of some kind. That it was an actual government ministry charged with confirming or denying the existence of ghosts occurred to no one. After all, who would credit such a thing in this day and age?

Off Bric-a-Brac Street ran another cobbled road called Prester Row. Along here were a few useful shops and businesses. There was a newspaper stand, a small supermarket, a fruit and vegetable shop called Shallots, a flower shop called Blossoms, a coffee shop called Beans, a butcher shop called Chops, and at the far end of the row, a fishmonger's named Good Coddley's. In addition, there was a barber shop called Trimmers and a ladies' hairdresser called Marlene's. Around the corner, in Blister Street, was Mr. Nostrum's Patent Remedies and a carpentry shop called The Legge Works.

Legge's carpentry works had been established in roughly the same era as the Ministry of Ghosts. It had originally specialized in the making of wooden legs for injured soldiers returning from the Battle of Waterloo.

The Legge Works had gone on making high quality wooden legs for many years and several generations, until the bottom finally fell out of the wooden leg market—due to lighter and better materials and scientific advancement.

The Legges had then gone on to banister-making and making chair legs, and then, latterly, making cricket and baseball bats—the skills needed to make good cricket bats not being so dissimilar to those required for making decent wooden legs. Obviously the shapes are not the same, but the principle is. To prove this, the present Mr. Legge's father, a cricketer himself, once scored a full century not out, while batting using one of his wooden legs as a substitute for a real bat. It had only been an exhibition match, but it had clearly vindicated his craftsmanship.

Now, the present Mr. Legge and his wife had two children, a toddler called May and an older child called Timber, who went to Eustace School. Timber was not his real name, which was Tim. But it was better than the nickname he used to have before, which was Knots.

Tim, or Timber (whichever you prefer, he answered to both), was a regular passerby along Bric-a-Brac Street. But he had never noticed the brass plate on the wall at the Ministry of Ghosts. And as he walked home that weekday afternoon—the afternoon of the day in which the Weekend Boy Wanted sign had gone up in the window—he was so engrossed in eating the gobstopper he had bought from Mrs. Hallet's Bon-Bons (for he kept taking the gobstopper out of his mouth to see whether it had changed color yet) that he failed to see the ad either.

Had he done so, he would have been interested. For he was an enterprising boy and not averse to working hard for a bit of money. He needed some cash, too, as he had a birthday present to buy soon—for himself. He always liked to buy himself a present on his birthday, on the principle that if you can't be nice to yourself and treat yourself on your birthday, how can you expect other people to?

So with his head down, and sucking on a gobstopper, Tim made his way past the Ministry of Ghosts. WEEK-END BOY WANTED, the sign read. FOR SATURDAYS ONLY. GOOD WAGES.

The hours would have suited young Tim, and so would the money; the promise of easy work and good wages would have lured him inside immediately. Had he seen the sign, he would have grasped the knocker and pummeled the door.

But he missed his chance—at least for the time being.

Yet the doorbell of the Ministry of Ghosts did ring that afternoon, and the knocker was knocked, too . . .

It was Mrs. Scant who heard it first, followed by her colleagues on the same floor, and then by old Mr. Copperstone, for the noise had roused him from his nap. "What on earth?"

The knocker was being knocked with an unheard of persistence—not to say, urgency, panic, anger, or indignation.

Mr. Gibbings went to a window and peered into the street to see who was creating the noise. Some troubled soul, he felt. Or someone with a grudge, bent on vengeance. He wasn't at all sure that the door should be opened to someone capable of creating such a racket. If they could do that with a piece of metal and a plank of wood, what other extreme acts were they capable of?

Yet, to Mr. Gibbings's surprise, he saw not the monster he had expected—someone of gorilla-like build and with immense paws where their hands should be.

No, it wasn't some huge ruffian he saw on the sidewalk, hammering at the door, and it wasn't a potential Weekend Boy either. It was a girl. A smallish one, too, who could barely reach the knocker and who was up on her tiptoes in order to be able to use it. In fact, she wasn't so much hammering the knocker as swinging from it and using her swings to give force to her summons. And by the look and the sound of it, she was not going to go away until that summons was responded to and the door was opened and it yielded to her will.

"What is that, Mr. Gibbings? For heaven's sake. It sounds like the end of the world has come."

Miss Rolly was next to him at the window.

"It appears to be a girl," he said. "Who seems to have her teeth into the knocker. I can't imagine what she wants."

"I think we'd better go and find out, don't you?" Miss Rolly said. "Before we all end up deaf."

"You don't suppose she's a ghost, do you?" Mr. Gibbings said hopefully.

"She looks a bit too solid to me," Miss Rolly said. "If that's a ghost then I'm a mint humbug."

Mr. Gibbings did not think that Miss Rolly looked anything like a mint humbug. Though he did think she was rather sweet sometimes.

Together they went out to the hall and together they opened the door. Mr. Copperstone looked down from the landing outside his office.

"Be careful!" he said. "They could be dangerous." Mrs. Scant stood back, close to the basement stairs, ready to run for it and perhaps to arm herself with a heavy teapot. At her feet, Boddington the cat waited—with his hair standing up on the back of his neck. He looked a bit like a big lizard. Or a small, furry dinosaur.

9

WEEKEND GIRL APPLIES

The name on the girl's shirt read EUSTACE, which was an odd name for a girl. She had a backpack hanging off one shoulder, which appeared to contain, judging from the lumps, some school books and a small ukulele.

Just as Mr. Gibbings was about to open the door, and the girl on the other side of it was about to give the brass knocker another hammering, the door appeared to swing open of its own accord. Presumably, Mr. Beeston had not properly secured it behind him when he had left.

The girl released her grip on the knocker, dropped to her feet, and looked defiantly at the figures in front of her—who, to her eyes, comprised of an old geezer (Mr. Copperstone), an unfashionable type (Mrs. Scant), a rather formidable lady (Miss Rolly), and a wimp (Mr. Gibbings).

"Good afternoon, young lady," the old geezer said. "Is there something we can do for you? You do seem to be creating the most appalling noise."

"I want to speak to somebody about this here notice," the girl said.

"What notice, young lady?" Mr. Copperstone said.

"This one here," the girl said, and she pointed to the notice in the window reading WEEKEND BOY WANTED.

"And what about it?" Mr. Copperstone asked.

"It's wrong," the girl said. "And what's more, it's not legal. I know my rights."

"I think you'd better come in for a moment," Mr. Copperstone said. "By the sound of it this isn't the sort of matter one can discuss on the doorstep."

"I'm not coming in unless you promise that I'll get out again," the girl said. "'Cause you all look a bit weird to me."

"Weird!" Mr. Copperstone said. "I will have you know, young lady, that we happen to be civil servants."

"Well, there you are then," the girl said. "That explains it. So, I'll come in, but don't try anything funny—"

"We wouldn't dream of it—" Mr. Copperstone said.

"I only live just down the road and around the corner."

"Do you now?"

"And if I don't get home they'll come looking for me."

"I'm sure they will, if they're dutiful parents."

"My dad owns Coddley's."

"Does he now?"

"Good Coddley's, the fish shop."

"Fish?"

"But just because we own a fish shop it doesn't mean we smell of herring."

"Absolutely not."

"In fact, all I ever smell of is fresh strawberries."

"Yes, indeed you do. Doesn't she, Mrs. Scant? Do you get that pleasant aroma wafting in your direction?"

"It's my soap."

"Very nice it is, too," Mrs. Scant said. "Fruity."

"It's strawberries."

"You said."

"So don't go saying I smell of herring."

"We wouldn't dream of it."

"All right then. I'll come in."

The girl did, and the door swung closed behind her.

"We'd better go to the conference room, I think," Mr. Copperstone said. "And hear what this young lady has to say."

"Well, I think you ought to take that notice down and bring it with you," the girl said. "As that's what we need to discuss."

"Really?" Mr. Copperstone said, both surprised by and impressed with this girl's level of assertiveness. "Then that's what we had better do. Mr. Gibbings, if you would be so kind . . ."

Mr. Gibbings went to fetch the notice. Mr. Copperstone led the way to the conference room—yet another dark and dingy room lined with books.

In appearance the girl was more robust than slender, yet she was not overly large. Perhaps compact was the word. She was not short, and yet neither was she tall. She was not exactly pretty, yet she was not plain, either. It sort of depended on the light and her mood perhaps. She could look quite angelic, and she could look equally as devilish.

"Please, take a seat."

The girl did. Her legs, when she sat down, did not quite reach the floor, so they dangled, and she swung them back and forth, as if she were warming up in order to kick someone.

"And may we inquire whom we have the pleasure of addressing, young lady?" Mr. Copperstone asked.

"Huh?" the girl said. "What are you saying?"

Mr. Copperstone actually blushed—or at least appeared to change color. Miss Rolly stepped in and said, "Your name. Mr. Copperstone was inquiring as to your name. I assume it isn't Eustace—even though that's the name on your shirt."

"Of course not. That's where I go to school. Who'd call a girl Eustace? You'd need to be crazy to do that."

This remark was greeted by a prolonged silence of disapproval; the civil service did not support or encourage this kind of observation.

"Anyway," the girl continued, aware of the frosty response but unabashed by it, "my name's Thruppence, if you want to know. And my last name's Coddley. As for my middle name, I haven't got one yet, but I might decide to have one at some point in the future. If so, I don't know what it will be, though I'm considering Mavis."

"I wouldn't choose Mavis," Mrs. Scant advised. "Sounds a bit . . . too old for you."

"Do you think so?" Thruppence Coddley said. "Then what about Bohemia?"

Mr. Copperstone cleared his throat. Mr. Gibbings had by now entered with the notice from the window.

"I think we're straying a little from the point," Mr. Copperstone went on. "Shall we stick to the business at hand?"

"What are you saying?" Thruppence Coddley said. She turned to Miss Rolly, who seemed to be the most sensible one. "What's he mean?"

"The notice," Miss Rolly said. "What did you want to say about it?"

"Oh yes," Thruppence Coddley said. "It's against the law, and it's showing discrimination."

"Showing what?" Mr. Gibbings said.

"You can't go putting notices up saying '*Weekend Boys Wanted.*'"

"I didn't," Mr. Gibbings said. "We only want one of them. It says '*Weekend Boy*'—singular."

"Not the point," Thruppence said. "What about Weekend Girls, huh? What about them?"

"Well, what about them?" Mr. Gibbings said.

"They're not getting a chance, are they?" Thruppence said. "You can't go putting notices up advertising jobs for Weekend Boys but not Weekend Girls. You have to say '*Weekend Persons Wanted.*'"

"Weekend Persons?" Mr. Gibbings said. "What's a Weekend Person? I've never heard of a Weekend Person ever!"

"Me, neither, I must confess," Mr. Copperstone said. "But maybe I'm out of touch."

"No, it has to be *Weekend Persons* or it has to be *Weekend Boy or Girl Wanted.*"

"Does it? Who says?" Mr. Gibbings asked.

"The law says," Thruppence Coddley said. "And I know my rights."

"I have no doubt of it," old Mr. Copperstone said. And he seemed to emit a long and weary sigh.

Mrs. Scant didn't appear very interested in what was going on, for the cat had come in and she was busy petting it. Miss Rolly, however, was highly alert and, moreover, sympathetic to the girl's cause. "I think this young lady is absolutely right, Mr. Gibbings," Miss Rolly said. "In fact, had you run this notice by me before putting it in the window, I would have pointed out the mistake and made exactly the same objection. Men and women and girls and boys should be treated equally. If a job is open to one, it should be open to the other. No question."

"But, Miss Rolly," Mr. Gibbings said, "when we consider the nature of the work—dare I say, the possibly dangerous nature of the work . . ."

Thruppence Coddley's eyes lit up, like lights on a Christmas tree. "Dangerous work, did you say?" she said. "I like dangerous work. What's it involve? I do dangerous work all the time. You should see me with the fish-gutting knife. Or getting mussels out of their shells. Not cut myself once or been carted off to the hospital ever. I thrive on danger, I do."

Mr. Copperstone peered at the girl over his half-moon glasses.

"Don't you like playing with dolls, young lady?" he said.

"I've got nothing against them," Thruppence told him. "But sharp knives are more exciting. And by the way, if any of you ever want any whelks or any jellied eels, my dad sells them at reasonable prices and very good they are, too."

"Well, maybe not just at the moment . . ." Mr. Copperstone said.

"In my opinion," Miss Rolly said, "we should do as this young lady suggests and reword the advertisement immediately."

"Mr. Gibbings?" Mr. Copperstone asked, one eyebrow raised in a question mark.

"No objection, sir," Mr. Gibbings said. "It wasn't deliberate. I just never thought it was the kind of job a girl might want to do. It's not that I'm against Weekend Girls as such. Not at all."

"Very well. We'll amend the notice, young lady, and then put it back in the window. Thank you for stopping by to bring the omission to our attention. Is there anything else we can do for you before you go?"

"Yes," Thruppence said. "This job—I'd like to apply for it."

There was a very long silence this time as the four adults looked around at each other then back at Thruppence Coddley then back at each other again.

"Well . . ." Mr. Copperstone said.

"I'm good at weekend jobs," Thruppence said.

"What weekend jobs have you done?"

"Fish gutting and cleaning lobsters," she said. "I can supply references."

"From whom?"

"My dad. But not from the lobsters."

"I'm not sure that references from relatives—"

"And my teacher. She'd give me one. She asked me to sift all the muck out of the sandpit once, and when I'd finished she said I'd done a marvelous job."

"Well, that is a recommendation, I suppose. Only ..."

"Only what?"

"Only, don't you want to know what the job is first?"

"All right, what is it then?"

"It isn't for the squeamish," Mr. Gibbings said.

"You can't do fish gutting and be squeamish," Thruppence pointed out.

"It's to do, you see ..." Mr. Copperstone said, "with ghosts."

"Ghosts?"

More silence. The adults watched the girl's face for her reaction, to see if it would be one of terror, of fear. But no.

"I like ghosts," Thruppence said. "That would suit me fine."

"Have you actually seen one then?" Mr. Copperstone said excitedly. "Do you have one at home that you could bring here in a jam jar?"

"No, well, I've never actually seen one. Just heard about them."

"Yes, we've all done that," Mrs. Scant said wearily. "Everyone's heard about them. But hearing isn't seeing, is it?"

"Yes," Miss Rolly said. "Because if you did have a ghost that would save us an enormous amount of trouble and inconvenience. It would even save us our jobs."

"Your jobs?" Thruppence said. "What do you mean?"

"Do you know where you are right now, young lady?" Mr. Copperstone said.

"Bric-a-Brac Street," Thruppence said.

"I mean, the nature of the building you are in?"

"Um . . . it's the government, isn't it?"

"It is the Ministry," Mr. Copperstone sighed, "of Ghosts."

Thruppence looked at him then she started to giggle then she said, "Get out of here. You're joking."

• • •

Over the course of the next ten minutes, Mr. Copperstone, Mrs. Scant, Miss Rolly, and Mr. Gibbings did their best to explain, as concisely and with as few diversions as possible, the history and purpose of the Ministry and the nature of the sticky situation in which they now found themselves. They further explained the theories of Grimes and Natterly's *Manual of Ghost Hunting*, expounding the apparent sensitivity of children and animals to the presence of ghosts. They could see and detect what adults could not. And they could even act as a kind of bait to lure ghosts in, due—possibly—to their open and non-judgmental natures. Whereas adults were more inclined to give a ghost a bad name and to think the worst of it.

When they were done, Thruppence Coddley sat quietly for a while, pondering what she had heard.

"So, basically you want someone to get you a ghost?"

"That's right. And we have three months in which to do it."

"You want someone to sort of . . . lure a ghost in?"

"That's it."

"Or to find one somewhere else and bring it to you?"

"That would be perfect."

"Hmm . . ." Thruppence said. "What's the money like?"

"Negotiable," Mr. Gibbings said.

"So, let's negotiate then," Thruppence said. "But you'd better know from the start that I don't even get out of bed for less than a tenner an hour."

"Ten pounds! Ten pounds an hour!" Mr. Copperstone was aghast. He clutched at his breast pocket and the general region of his heart.

"Though I may consider coming down a bit," Thruppence said. "Depending."

"On what?"

"Circumstances," she said vaguely.

"Well, you would need to put in a formal application," Mr. Gibbings said.

"I just have."

"I felt that was rather *in*formal, myself."

"It's as formal as you're going to get," Thruppence said. "I don't really do formal. I'm not filling out pages of application forms and all that business. Not just for a weekend job."

"Well, we are obliged," Mr. Copperstone said, "to advertise any job for at least forty-eight hours, under Ministry rules. So we'll have to put the amended sign up in the window, in case there are other applicants. Then we'll be able to make a decision. So, in the meantime, if you'd care to leave your name with us . . ."

"I'll need it, won't I?" Thruppence said.

"Pardon?"

"My name. I'll be needing it, so how can I leave it with you? I can't go home with no name, can I? No one'll know what to call me. They'll just say, 'Here's whatsher-face back from school,' and they won't know who I am."

"No, I didn't mean leave your name in that sense, I meant . . . we'll just make a note of your name and your interest in the position, and we'll advertise for another day or so, and . . . and we'll be in touch."

Thruppence looked dubious, as if there were some kind of swindle going on, but she couldn't quite put her finger on what it was.

"Well, all right then, I suppose. I'll write it down for you." They gave her a pen and paper. "There," she said, when she had finished. "Thruppence Coddley, Good Coddley's Fish Shop. Just Around the Corner From Here. And I've written my cell number, as well as my home number, if you need to give me a call."

"Cell number?" old Mr. Copperstone said. "And what might that be? Were you once in prison?"

Thruppence looked at the other three civil servants as if to say, "Is he for real?" and they returned her gaze with what she assumed were sympathetic glances, as though they all knew and accepted that Mr. Copperstone was getting on in years and no longer at the cutting edge.

"Okay then," Thruppence said. "You've got my details, if you need to get in touch. But if anyone can find you a ghost, it'll be me. I'm not scared of much, and even when I am, I can handle it. So no worries on that account. I'm quite happy to go looking for ghosts anywhere, up the bell tower, down at the cemetery, at the crematorium, wherever. And don't forget, if you want some whelks for your tea, my dad's got the best whelks for miles. And if anyone ever tells you I smell of herring, they're lying, as I don't, 'cause I only ever smell of strawberries, and all my friends can tell you that, so there."

With those remarks, Thruppence hopped down from the chair, picked up her bag, and indicated that the interview was over, for she was a busy girl with much to do and with plenty of whelks on her plate.

"I'll see you to the door," Miss Rolly said.

"No need, I know the way," Thruppence said.

But Miss Rolly went with her. At the front door, as Thruppence was leaving, she called after her and said, "Thruppence . . ."

"Yes?"

"I admire your spunk. We girls must stick together and fight for equality. Onwards and upwards, Thruppence. Onwards and upwards for women's rights!"

And the hitherto rather humorless and somewhat surly Thruppence gave a wide and rather wonderfully engaging smile. It was like the sun coming out on a cloudy day.

"I wasn't too rough with them, was I?" she said.

"Not a bit," Miss Rolly told her. "You were just right." And she, too, gave a sunshine smile, and they grinned at each other like conspirators, hitherto unknown to each other, and surprised and yet delighted to find themselves in the same conspiracy. "I'll put a word in for you," Miss Rolly promised. "If someone else applies for the job, too, I'll try to make sure you get it."

"Thank you," Thruppence said. "I'd better go. Got homework to do."

"Bye then," Miss Rolly said.

"Bye."

Thruppence went on her way, and Miss Rolly closed the door, and in the vestibule of the Ministry was the faint aroma of strawberries—but in a way, it was more than that; it was also like a breath of fresh air.

10

ANOTHER JOB SEEKER

The door knocker of the Ministry of Ghosts had rested unused, and the panels of the door had stood unbattered, for many a long year. Visitors were few and callers were scarce, and of casual inquirers, there had been none for decades.

But now, within the space of as many days, two people had employed both bell and door knocker to attract the attention of those within, and here, upon the third day, was yet another.

It was morning, and the day was fresh, and the Ministry had only just opened. But already there were callers and seekers of attention.

Again? Mr. Copperstone thought, as the sound of rapping rose up to his sanctum. *More callers? It is getting busy. First that obnoxious Beeston, then that rather spirited Thruppence girl, and now today, yet more summonses to the door. We are getting popular. My, oh my. It's positively rush hour.*

Yet, while Mr. Copperstone thought these thoughts, he had no intention of acting upon them. If some caller wished to be admitted, it was not his job to open the door. He was too important for that. He was, after all, a very senior civil servant, and opening doors was a matter for the lower staff.

"I'll get it," Mr. Gibbings called. He left his desk and headed for the hall, but Miss Rolly and Mrs. Scant were already there. In truth, they all felt rather stimulated by this sudden influx of callers, for it made them feel significant, and at the center of things after so many quiet years of peripheral inactivity and, well, boredom.

"Things are heating up here, aren't they, Miss Rolly?" Mr. Gibbings said, as they all made their way to the front door.

"We seem to be in demand all of a sudden. We're quite the business these days here at the Ministry."

"Yes, Mr. Gibbings," Miss Rolly said, somewhat loftily. She felt that Mr. Gibbings's puppy-like enthusiasm was rather juvenile and lacking in proper bureaucratic solemnity.

Mrs. Scant was already at the door, with her fingers reaching toward the handle. The door pulled back—it seemed to be creaking a little less loudly than usual—and it opened wide to reveal a boy on the step. He was somewhat freckled, but not excessively, and while he looked very clean, he did have something of the air of an unmade bed about him. This was by no means due to lack of hygiene or scarcity of soap, so much as from a natural propensity toward untidiness.

"'Ello," the boy said.

"It's a boy," Miss Rolly said to Mr. Gibbings in a low voice.

"A small one."

"Yes, I've seen them before," Mr. Gibbings confided.

"So have I," Miss Rolly said. "But never with so much shirt sticking out or with so much hair standing up in all directions."

The boy was wearing a sweatshirt with the word Eustace on the front—just as Thruppence Coddley had worn the previous afternoon. So the three adults staring at him now knew enough to understand that this was unlikely to be his own name but referred to the school that he attended.

"What can we do for you, young man?" Mrs. Scant said.

"If you're here to clean the chimney, I'm afraid we're no longer using coal, as we have switched over to gas. So chimney sweeping is no longer needed. Though, if you are looking for something useful to do, you can always polish the old coal scuttle." The boy looked at her with an expression on his face that clearly revealed (a) he thought she was a bit batty, and (b) he had no idea what she was talking about.

"I'm here about the job," he said. "The one posted in the window."

"Oh, another applicant!" Mrs. Scant said. "The second in two days."

"Your sign there," the boy said, "that says *Weekend Girl or Boy Person Required for Saturdays*. I'd like to apply for the job."

"Is it another jobseeker down there?" Mr. Copperstone's reedy voice came piping down the stairs, followed by his elderly limbs and the rest of him.

"It is, Mr. Copperstone," Miss Rolly answered.

"Then let us have a look at the fellow," Mr. Copperstone said. He proceeded to do that.

"So, it's a boy this time, is it? Might I ask your name, young chap?"

"Tim," the boy said. "Tim Legge. I live just around the corner. Well, a couple of corners, really, and then down a lane. We've got a shop there. The Legge Works. We started off selling wooden legs but now it's bats. They play with our cricket bats in the test matches."

"Oh, cricket!" old Mr. Copperstone said. "I used to watch a lot of cricket when I was a younger man. You can't beat cricket. You can sit down and sleep through it all day long."

"We made banisters as well once," the boy said. "But you can't play cricket with them. Not generally speaking. Though I suppose you could if you had to. Anyway, I'm on my way to school and I'm probably going to be late now, but I wanted to get my application in quick and beat the rush. I'm especially interested in the good wages, as I've got to earn some so I can buy somebody a birthday present."

"How kind and thoughtful," Miss Rolly said. "Who are you buying a present for? A sibling? Your dear mama?"

"No," Tim Legge said. "Me."

"You?"

"It's a sort of tradition," Tim said. "Every year, around the time of my birthday, I get myself a present. I feel I deserve it. And there's only a few months to go. So I need to save up fast. What are the hours, and when can I start?"

"Now hold on, young man," Mr. Gibbings said. "It's not quite that simple."

"Yes, don't you want to know what the job is first?" Mr. Copperstone said. "Before submitting a formal application?"

"Then we may need to call up references," Miss Rolly said.

"And have a cup of tea," Mrs. Scant added.

"And we already have other applicants under consideration," Miss Rolly said. "A rather personable young lady, whom we are quite partial to. In fact, she is top of our list right now."

"Though she is the only one on it," Mr. Gibbings pointed out.

"Be that as it may—" Miss Rolly said.

"All right, what is the job?" Tim Legge said. "Tell me a bit about it, then I'll send in my application."

"It's to do with ghosts," Mr. Gibbings said, and this time he was very solemn and very serious, too.

"Ghosts and catching them," Miss Rolly said. "It's not work for the fainthearted or for those of a delicate constitution or for mama's boys."

Tim Legge looked indignant.

"Who's saying I'm a mama's boy?" he demanded. "You show them to me and I'll knock their front teeth out."

"Well, there's no reason to go to extremes," Mr. Copperstone said. "I'm sure that we don't need to be doing any dentistry as such—"

"Just saying that I'm not no mama's boy," the boy said. "And I'm not afraid of a few ghosts, either. I eat ghosts for breakfast, I do."

"Don't you have cereal and toast though?" Mrs. Scant said. "Washed down with a nice cup of tea?"

"I think he was speaking metaphorically, Mrs. Scant," Mr. Copperstone said.

"Oh, was he now?" Mrs. Scant said wonderingly. "Just think of it. I never heard of boys doing that before."

"So, where are the ghosts then?" Tim Legge demanded. "You just show them to me, and I'll take care of them. I'll bag them up for you in no time and chuck them in the trash."

"No, no," Mr. Copperstone said. "You're grasping the wrong end of the stick, young man. We need a Weekend Boy—"

"Or Girl—" Miss Rolly interrupted.

"Quite right. We need a Weekend Boy or Girl to find a ghost for us. For—in case you didn't read the brass plate—we are the Ministry of Ghosts. But, sadly, neither we nor our predecessors have been able to find a ghost in over two hundred years. If we don't find one soon, we'll be closed down."

"And redeployed to the Sewage Department," Mr. Gibbings said.

"That is, those of us who are not being forcibly retired," Mr. Copperstone said.

Then they all began to talk at once.

"And we've only got three months to do it."

"And according to Grimes and Natterly's *Manual of Ghost Hunting*—"

"Which you are no doubt familiar with."

"It is on the school curriculum, one assumes—"

"Children are more sensitive to the presence of ghosts than adults—"

"And can even lure them—"

"Acting as a kind of bait, or temptation, as it were."

"So you just get us a ghost, young man, and not only will you be able to buy yourself a birthday present—"

"We'll send you a card, too."

"So how does that sound?"

They fell silent and waited for some reaction from the untidy boy on the step.

"What does it pay?" he said.

"Minimum wage," Mrs. Scant said.

"I wouldn't work for less," the boy said. "No way."

"Nobody should be expected to," Mrs. Scant agreed. "You should never work for less than the minimum. Stands to reason."

"I'll think about it," the boy said.

"So will we," Miss Rolly said.

"Now that I know what the job is, I'm not so sure I want it," Tim Legge said.

"Well, we may not want you," Miss Rolly pointed out. "For we already have one other applicant and may yet have several more."

"It's early in the search," Mrs. Scant said.

"Very early," Mr. Gibbings agreed. "Early in the search and early in the day. All the pupils from your school might still apply. Who knows?"

"Well, I was here first," Tim Legge said.

"Second, actually," Miss Rolly said.

"All right, I want to apply for the job then."

"Then leave us your card and we shall consider your application and we will be in touch," Mr. Copperstone said.

"Don't have a card," Tim said.

"Oh. That is inconvenient."

"Just leave us your name then," Mr. Gibbings said.

"Leave you my name? But what if I need it and I've left it with you? No one'll know who I am!"

"For heaven's sake," Mr. Copperstone said. "Don't they teach you at your school that when you leave your name you don't actually leave your name; all you do is leave your name. That girl said exactly the same thing."

"What girl?" Tim said.

"She said her name was Thruppence."

"Thruppence Coddley?"

"That was her."

"Who never smells of fish?"

"Only strawberries, apparently," Mr. Gibbings said.

"She's in my class," Tim said.

"How do we know you're not in hers?" Miss Rolly asked.

"Same difference," Tim said.

"Is it though?" Miss Rolly said. "How do we know it's not a different difference?"

"Aren't we splitting hairs here?" Mr. Copperstone said.

"Might be, might not," Tim Legge said cryptically. "And anyway, you can't trust her," he continued. "Thruppence Coddley will never find a ghost for you. She couldn't find a wooden leg in a wooden leg factory."

"Why not?" Miss Rolly said, feeling that she should champion Thruppence Coddley's side.

"She just couldn't, that's all. She wouldn't know where to start. Girls aren't good at finding ghosts. Boys are good at that. Especially boys called Tim. Everyone knows that."

"I didn't," Mrs. Scant said.

"Well, there you go," Tim said nonchalantly. "I guess it's true that we all learn something new every day. Anyhow, time's passing—"

"Indeed it is," Mr. Copperstone said. "I have ever found that to be the case, despite my advanced age . . . Time has passed me by for several years now, and I dare say it will continue to do so, until the end—"

"And I'd better get to school or I'll be late and get into trouble. Not that I mind a bit of trouble, personally," Tim said.

"But all things in moderation," Mrs. Scant said.

"Yeah," Tim said. "You don't want to have too much trouble or you won't have time for anything else. So I shall leave you my name like you said, and then if I do need it for anything, I can always come back and you can return it. Or if I forget it, you can tell me what it is."

Mr. Copperstone sighed.

"Mr. Gibbings, would you take a note of the young man's name and address and telephone number?"

"Of course, sir."

He did, and the brief doorstep interview was over.

"Okay, well, you'll let me know then will you, guys?" Tim Legge said.

The four civil servants stared at him in a kind of incredulous horror. Guys? Had this boy just addressed old and eminent Mr. Copperstone and forceful Miss Rolly and young Mr. Gibbings and the ever purposeful Mrs.

Scant as guys? Guys! What was the world coming to? Guys, indeed. It was unheard of, unprecedented, unbelievable.

"Y-yes, yes. I-I suppose we will," Mr. Copperstone managed to stutter.

"Okay. Gotta go. Catch you later then, guys. You all chill, now. And don't forget, if it's ghosts you want then I'm the dude. And if you ever want a new cricket bat, my dad'll give you a discount. High fives then, huh, guys!"

Tim Legge would definitely have given the assembled civil servants high fives all around, but they seemed not to know what he was talking about and just stared at him in open-mouthed bewilderment.

"No? Okay. Suit yourselves. Catch you later then. Gotta split!"

With that, and with his backpack, his sticking-up hair, and his general air of being made from several irregular bits of cardboard randomly stuck together, Tim Legge went on his way, and he started to whistle as he went.

Mr. Copperstone looked at his underlings.

"Guys? Dudes? High fives?" he said. He shook his head slowly and sorrowfully. "It wasn't like that in my day. Whatever are we to do?"

"How about a cup of tea, sir?" Mrs. Scant said.

"A fabulous idea, Mrs. Scant," Mr. Copperstone said.

"Then, perhaps, we can convene in my office to discuss our next step."

They did convene to do so. Yet somehow—as ever—the promised tea did not appear. Nobody liked to mention it. But it was certainly a mystery, Mrs. Scant and her tea. She was always about to make it, she was always offering to make it, and she frequently seemed to think that she had made it. But the kettle never quite boiled somehow, the cups never got as far as the tray, the cookies remained in the packet, and the tea just never arrived.

It made you wonder sometimes. It really did. Just what was going on.

11

THE SUCCESSFUL CANDIDATE

When weekends came, the Ministry of Ghosts seemed a hollow, bereft, lonely, and deserted place.

Saturdays, public holidays, long Sunday afternoons—they all took their toll and appeared to leave a little more dust on the windows, a little more darkness within, a little more discoloration on the ancient, brass nameplate.

Few people passed along Bric-a-Brac Street between Friday night and Monday morning. The schools were closed, as were any neighboring offices, and those seeking pleasure and entertainment and shopping opportunities would not have selected the Bric-a-Brac route, for there were far more interesting thoroughfares in other areas, where the bright shops sparkled with window displays and where the movie theaters offered the choice of a dozen films.

But in Bric-a-Brac Street there was silence. No sight of Mr. Copperstone. No sound of Miss Rolly. Not a glimpse of Mr. Gibbings. Not a word from Mrs. Scant. Of course, they must have had lives of their own, homes to go to, meals to cook and to eat, hobbies to pursue, friends and relations to visit, bookshelves to put up, and holes to drill in walls.

Yet, it was also hard to imagine them away from the place, so steeped were they in its dusty aura. The Ministry of Ghosts and those who worked there seemed inseparable in some ways, as if the place and the people had grown into each other and had become one.

Tick then *tock*. The clock in the hallway tolled the passing of time. It marked the minutes and mourned the hours with a weary chime. Motes of dust still hung in the sunlight, slowly falling. Where did all the dust come from? When did the cleaners arrive to vacuum it all away?

Tock, and then *tick*. Little by little, minute by interminable minute, the long, long weekend leaked away. Outside, away from Bric-a-Brac Street, were crowds and commotion, gaiety and laughter, movement and vitality, and the throb of life. But here, just shade and shadow, and some inner rooms, impenetrable to sunlight, and occasionally, from the direction of the basement, the meow of a cat. Boddington, no doubt, with a weekend's supply of food and water left for him somewhere, you would suppose, and with his own personal cat door in one of the doors, allowing him to escape on his adventures.

As for the ghosts—the ghosts that the Ministry had been set up to find—where were they? Were they all merely illusions in the minds of the credulous and the gullible? Were they little more than stories to be told around campfires, with the small flames burning and the woodsmoke rising, and the darkness behind you, and the fear growing, and your spine tingling as the storyteller wove his fantastic cloth of impossible, improbable, yet dazzlingly colorful yarns?

Ghosts. Maybe there was not a single one and never had been. And all this work, this seeking, this believing, this fear, this appeasement, this terror of the unknown, and this eternal wondering about what lay beyond life's end—it was all for nothing.

In truth, maybe all that lay on the other side of life was peace and quiet and silence and the long shadows and the dust falling—something like the inside of the Ministry of Ghosts, during those long, monotonous, everlasting weekends.

• • •

Suddenly, now, a sound is heard. A telephone is ringing. It echoes throughout the building. Its noise is heard in every room. Who can it be? Who would call the Ministry of Ghosts so late on a Saturday evening?

Down in the basement, Boddington swivels his yellow eyes. What's that? Who's there? What do they want? What's happening? Is it news? Disaster? Celebration? Change? The ending of an old era? The start of a new? Isn't someone going to pick up the phone? Isn't someone going to answer? You can't expect a cat to—

The telephone goes on ringing. The curtains try to muffle the sound, but cannot silence it. *Hush, hush*, the dark wood paneling seems to say. Not here. Not now. This is the Ministry and is not to be disturbed.

The phone falls silent. The whole building seems to sigh its relief. But before it can settle back to its slumbers, the phone starts to ring again. It's even louder now, surely, like a rooster crowing in the early morning, commanding the hens, the chickens, the farm, the farmer, the country-side, the whole county, to wake up, up, up—now!

Can't someone do something to stop it? It's all surely a mistake anyway. A wrong number. A hoax call. A prank. An automated call from one of those infernal businesses that are always calling to sell you new windows or in-surance. It can't be a real call. Not a real call. No one ever calls the Ministry of Ghosts at this hour—not on a weekend. They haven't done so for years, for decades, not once in living memory nor in the memory of the dead, either—if they still have memories.

For heaven's sake—STOP!

And it does. It's like a toothache ending. The bad molar extracted. Relief. Pain gone. Silence resumes, like a settling bird finding a branch now and folding its wings. It tilts its head, closes its eyes, puffs up the cushion of its feathers. It sleeps. The whole building sleeps. Desks and carpets and tables and chairs. All asleep. Look into my eyes; you feel yourself grow heavy; your eyelids feel heavy; there is nothing you can do; you cannot help your-self; you must sleep, sleep, sleep.

And when the building wakes, it is Monday morn-ing again. The weekend is gone to wherever it is that weekends go. The garbage truck that removes the resi-due of old weekends has come and collected the trash and has taken it to the dump. There it rests, with all the other weekends past, perhaps one day to be recycled and turned into fresh, new time.

• • •

"Mr. Copperstone, sir."

"Mrs. Scant. Good morning to you."

"At your desk already, sir?"

"Such is the fate of the man at the top, Mrs. Scant. The last to leave and the first to arrive and always the one to go down with the sinking ship. Not that we're sinking yet—I hope."

"I certainly hope not, sir. Did you have a good weekend?"

"Quiet, Mrs. Scant, but pleasant enough. And yourself?"

"Yes, very nice, sir. Quiet, too, but all very restful."

"That's it, Mrs. Scant. Recharge the batteries, huh?"

"Try to relax, sir, that's it."

"Ah. Do I hear voices?"

"Miss Rolly and Mr. Gibbings, by the sound of it, sir. They often get in at the same time."

"Good, good. Then we're all here and all punctual and ready to get down to another hard day's work."

Mrs. Scant looked doubtful. She might have asked Mr. Copperstone how many years it had been now since he had last done a hard day's work. But that would have been tactless and not very sensible, so she refrained and simply inquired, "Shall I make a pot of tea, sir?"

"If you could, Mrs. Scant. That would be greatly appreciated."

So off Mrs. Scant went to put the kettle on, greeting Mr. Gibbings and Miss Rolly on her way.

"I'm putting the kettle on," she told them, "if you'd like a cup."

"Lovely," Mr. Gibbings said.

"Thanks very much," Miss Rolly said. "Very kind of you." She headed for her office and listened out for the sound of tea.

• • •

Around eleven that morning, Mr. Copperstone "summoned the troops," as he put it, to discuss the matter of the Weekend Boy (or Girl).

"I think," he said, "that we need to make a decision soon as to whom we shall offer the job. Who do we think is the most suitable candidate? Perhaps it would be best to first make a shortlist."

"It's short already," Miss Rolly pointed out. 'There are only two names on it. If we shortened it any further, there would only be one on it. If we shortened it beyond that, there would be nobody on it. And we can hardly offer *them* the job—nobody."

Mr. Copperstone thought this over. He nodded.

"Good point, Miss Rolly. So there have been no other applicants for the position?"

"No, sir," Miss Rolly said. "And I don't think we can afford to wait much longer. We've only got three months to find a ghost. Less than three months now, as it was already last week that Mr. Beeston was here."

"True, true."

"Time is—" Miss Rolly began.

"Of the essence!" Mr. Gibbings completed. Then he appeared to blush.

"Okay then. Let's have your opinions," Mr. Copperstone said. "Who's in favor of offering the job to the boy? And who's in favor of the girl?"

"I feel there is something to be said for both of them," Mrs. Scant said. "The girl did seem very competent, and she did smell nicely of strawberries. But then the boy seemed very bright, too, and sounds like he knows what he's doing—"

"I think the girl should be given an opportunity," Miss Rolly said. "It's time that women got the chance to succeed and—"

"I quite agree," Mrs. Scant said, "only what if we offered the job to both of them?"

Mr. Copperstone was astonished. "Both of them?"

"Many hands." Mrs. Scant nodded. "Light work. Two heads," she said. "Better than one."

"Too many cooks," Miss Rolly said, "spoil the broth."

"A stitch in time," Mr. Gibbings said, not wishing to be left out, "saves nine."

"Quite—" said Mr. Copperstone.

"Yes, I think employing them both would be ideal," Mrs. Scant interrupted. "That way, we get the best of both worlds. I mean, some ghosts might appear to girls, but not to boys. Some to boys, but not to girls. So, if we have one of each, we double our chances."

"But can we afford to employ two ghost hunters?" Mr. Copperstone said. "How are the accounts, Miss Rolly?" he asked.

"I think we can manage it, sir," she said. "Petty cash is . . . well . . . we've not spent anything out of the petty cash fund in a while. We are positively overflowing with it."

"Positively overflowing, are we?" Mr. Copperstone said. "Well, it's good to be overflowing, especially with money."

"We could even afford to pay them a bonus if they find any ghosts."

"You mean . . . ?"

"Yes, sir. If they catch a ghost for us, we can give them a bit extra."

"That is an incentive," Mr. Copperstone said. "Very well. I'm in favor of Mrs. Scant's suggestion. What do you think?"

"If we can afford it . . ." Mr. Gibbings said.

"I suppose there's nothing to lose," Miss Rolly agreed.

"Very well. We'll offer them both positions as ghost catchers. We'll have a Weekend Boy accompanied by a Weekend Girl. When shall we ask them to start?"

"How about Saturday?" Mr. Gibbings suggested.

Mr. Copperstone demurred. "Yes, we could, I suppose," he said. "Only Saturday is rather a long way away. It is Monday now and that means waiting until, well . . . the end of the week. And as Miss Rolly pointed out earlier, time is—"

"Of the essence!" Mr. Gibbings said then realized he had interrupted once more and became embarrassed again.

"Right. We need to get going as soon as possible. Perhaps we could ask them to start today."

"They'll be at school, sir," Miss Rolly pointed out.

"Yes . . . hmm . . . but maybe they could still do a bit of work after school and in the evenings. Once they've done their homework. Obviously that must take priority. We'll see what they say. So—Miss Rolly, Mr. Gibbings— would you be able to contact them and offer them the positions to start immediately?"

"Of course, sir. We have their phone numbers. We can leave messages for them to stop by after school on their way home."

But the messages were not necessary, for both Thruppence Coddley and Tim "Timber" Legge had independently decided that they would go to the Ministry of Ghosts on their way home from school that day, to discover if their job applications had been successful.

• • •

So it was that Thruppence Coddley, in her sweatshirt reading EUSTACE, and with her backpack on her shoulder, stood at the front door of the Ministry of Ghosts about to give the knocker another of her formidable pummelings, when she saw Tim Legge coming up the street. And instead of going past, when he saw her, he stopped.

"Hello," he said. "What are you doing here?"

"Nothing," she said. "You?"

"Nothing," he said. "Just admiring the scenery."

"Me, too," Thruppence said, and they both looked up and down the street in an admiring way.

Then they both sat on the step, each willing the other to disappear.

"Oh, look," Tim said, after a while, twisting his head around to see the window. "There's a sign up there saying '*Weekend Boy or Girl Person Wanted.*' I wonder what that's about."

"Hmm," Thruppence said. "I wonder." Then she lost her patience and said, "Look here, Tim Legge, I've applied for that job and I want to find out if I've gotten it, so why don't you go home and let me do what I came here for?"

Tim looked at her with indignation.

"You?" he said. "You've applied for the job?"

"Yes."

"You know what this place is, don't you?"

"Of course I do."

"This is the Ministry of Ghosts."

"I am quite aware—"

"And they're looking for a ghost catcher. A ghost lurer, even. Who'll lure them in and trap 'em."

"So?"

"Well, that's not a job for girls," Tim said. "That's a job for boys."

"Who says?" Thruppence said. "It's a job for whoever can do it. And I can!"

"I don't think so," Tim said. "Girls see ghosts and they run off screaming. Or is it the other way around?"

"Boys see ghosts and they wet their pants," Thruppence said.

"Not this boy," said Tim. "And I'm not moving."

"Me neither," Thruppence said.

And there they might have sat indefinitely, waiting for each other to go home, had the door behind them not swung open, seemingly of its own accord. When they turned, there was Mrs. Scant, smiling down at them, saying, "I thought I heard voices. So there you are. It's our two candidates. Our Weekend Girl and our Weekend Boy. Do come in, both, won't you? Mr. Copperstone is waiting to see you."

The two children entered together. There was no "after you." They squeezed in side by side, elbow to elbow. The big door closed behind them, and Mrs. Scant led the way up the stairs. They followed her up to Mr. Copperstone's sanctum, where Miss Rolly and Mr. Gibbings were also waiting and they were warmly greeted with welcoming smiles.

12
A DEAL

I'm afraid there's no cake. But we might have a cookie around here," Mrs. Scant said.

"It's fine, thank you, Mrs. Scant," Mr. Copperstone said. "I think we'll just continue with the matter in hand." He, thus—to the children's mutual disappointment—declined on their behalf.

It felt like a visit to the school principal (just as Mr. Copperstone had once felt). Not that Thruppence or Tim had ever behaved so badly that they had been summoned to see the principal. But it felt that way. The room, the dark pictures on the walls of ancient civil servants from long ago, wearing wing collars and buttoned up coats; the leather chairs; the wooden paneling; the searching eyes of Mr. Copperstone, Miss Rolly, Mrs. Scant, and Mr. Gibbings. It felt like less of an interview and more of an interrogation.

"It'll be good cop, bad cop. You wait and see," Tim Legge whispered to Thruppence.

"It'll be what?" she said.

Before Tim could elaborate, Mr. Copperstone cleared his throat, which seemed to be his custom prior to important announcements.

"Ahem. Now, then. The fact is, children—if I may call you that?"

It seemed fair enough in the circumstances, so the two children nodded.

"The fact is that we have had quite an influx of applicants for the job in question, as Weekend Boy—"

"Or Girl," Miss Rolly reminded him.

"I was about to say that, Miss Rolly, have no fear. Yes, we have had an influx of two applicants."

"Doesn't sound like much of an influx to me," Tim Legge said. "I thought influxes were like downpours."

"Or floods," Thruppence added. "Not much of an influx when there's just the two of you. More like a trickle, I'd say."

"Maybe so," Mr. Copperstone said. "Maybe not so. However, we have decided to offer both of you the job. You both seem to have exemplary and complementary qualities. So what do you say?"

They didn't need long to think about it.

"No, thanks," Tim Legge said. "I'm not going to be a Weekend Girl for any amount of money."

"No, you—" Mr. Copperstone tried to say.

"And I'm not working as a Weekend Boy," Thruppence said. "I'm not doing that. That's a sort of job for an idiot or a halfwit. I'm not getting involved in that kind of thing. I've got my social standing to think of."

"Hang on," Tim said. "What do you mean . . . ?"

"No, you misunderstand me," Mr. Copperstone said. "Plainly the young lady would get the Weekend Girl job, and the young gentleman, the—"

"Oh, right. I see. That's not so bad then," Tim said. "But we wouldn't have to share the wages, would we?"

"No, no. Full wages for each position."

"And all we have to do is produce a couple of ghosts?"

"One would do," Mr. Gibbings said.

"Half of one, if that's all that you can manage," Mrs. Scant said.

"Though a whole one would be better," Miss Rolly said.

"Hmm," Tim said.

"Hmm," Thruppence agreed.

"And how would we get a hold of those ghosts, exactly?" Tim asked.

"Well, that's up to you," Mr. Copperstone said. "Though you would have full access to the library, to all our ghost hunting books and implements, and to everything in the muniments."

"What's muniments?" Tim said.

"It's like—an archive," Mr. Copperstone explained.

"What's an archive?" Tim asked.

"It's like—muniments," Mr. Copperstone said.

"So what's mun—?"

"I think we're going around in circles a little," Miss Rolly said.

"What's circles?" Tim said, with an unappreciated stab at humor.

"The archive is where we store all our files and records. You'll find some very valuable information in there," Miss Rolly said, "to help you entrap a ghost. It's true that we've tried all the methods for ourselves, and for us, they didn't work. But we're not children. And if Grimes and Natterly are to be believed—"

"And how could they not be believed?" Mr. Gibbings said. "When their *Manual of Ghost Hunting* is the very bible and textbook of the trade!"

"Yes indeed," Miss Rolly allowed. "But if Grimes and Natterly are to be believed—"

"And I think they are—"

"Yes, I think we have established that, Mr. Gibbings."

"I beg your pardon."

"If they are to be believed then a child may succeed where an adult will fail. Children can open doors to the spirit world that are closed to their elders, such abilities gone—if I may get poetic for a moment—like lost innocence, or like winter snow vanished from the fields."

"Very moving description," Mr. Copperstone said. "You brought a little tear to the eye."

"Thank you, sir."

"Not at all."

"So," Miss Rolly said, "you will have full access to all the information we possess. We will help you both in any way we can, and any equipment you need will be provided on expenses. Though we do have quite a lot of ghost hunting and ghost trapping implements already down in the utility room."

"Can we see it?" Thruppence asked.

Miss Rolly glanced at Mr. Copperstone.

"Of course," he said. "A perfectly reasonable request. Let us all go down there, and Miss Rolly can give us the tour."

Up they all rose and traipsed down the stairs, following Miss Rolly to the storage room in the basement. They got a quick glimpse of Boddington on the way before he darted out of sight. But he didn't seem to have any dead rats with him, which was both a good thing and a slight disappointment.

"Here we are," Miss Rolly said, flinging open the door. Well, maybe the hinges were too rusty and unoiled for the door to be actually flung open, but it parted company with the frame after a little persuasion.

"Coh!" Tim said. "It's like Aladdin's cave."

"So many things!" Thruppence said. "What do they all do?"

"Catch ghosts," Mr. Gibbings said. "In theory. Though in practice . . ."

There were apparatus everywhere. There were jars and containers and boxes of clothes. There were bells and books and candles. There were lures—the kind you might use in fly fishing—and nets.

"What good are nets for ghosts?" Thruppence said. "Won't they slip right through them?"

But nets were just a part of it. There were tubes and goggles and protective clothing and thick, fireproof gloves.

There were gas masks and breathing apparatus and tanks of oxygen. There was even a gun.

"It only fires blanks," Mr. Copperstone explained. "For getting rid of troublesome ghosts. They don't like noise or explosions."

And in a corner, in a container marked with a skull and crossbones, was a wooden box labeled DYNAMITE.

Next to the dynamite was a powerful-looking vacuum cleaner, its hose running into a reinforced steel tank.

"For sucking them up," Mr. Copperstone said. "And then making sure they can't escape."

Hanging from a hook were some bulbs of garlic.

"In case of vampires. Though we've not been troubled by them as of yet."

"What if, while looking for a ghost, we come across a vampire instead?" Tim asked.

"Oh . . ." Mr. Copperstone looked at his staff for opinions.

"Let it go, I think, sir," Mr. Gibbings said.

"I think so, too," Mrs. Scant said.

And Miss Rolly nodded.

"We are the Ministry of Ghosts, after all. Not the Ministry of Vampires."

"Is there a Ministry of Vampires?" Mr. Copperstone said.

"There ought to be," Mrs. Scant said. "And a Ministry of Werewolves. Big, hairy things out there baying at the moon of an evening and curdling your milk."

"Yes, anyway, no vampires, thank you," Mr. Copperstone said. "Just ghosts."

"Well, there seems to be everything here," Tim Legge said, opening the lid of a coffin that was standing up in a corner. "What's this for?"

"We were hoping a ghost without a home might like it," Mr. Gibbings said. "So we left it ajar with a pie inside to tempt the ghost in. But it didn't work."

"What happened to the pie?" Thruppence asked.

"I think the cat ate it," Mr. Gibbings said.

"Well, if you've seen everything," Mr. Copperstone said, "shall we go back upstairs and talk terms?"

"Terms?" Tim said.

"Pay," Mr. Copperstone said.

"Oh. Those sorts of terms. Right."

• • •

Thruppence Coddley and Tim Legge were tough negotiators, and they made it clear that they were not going to work for peanuts. But with a bit of give and take on either side, an agreement was soon reached. The two children would receive the adult minimum wage rate, per hour, plus all expenses, plus substantial bonuses for each ghost caught—up to a maximum of five ghosts. Any ghosts above that number would not be required, but the two ghost catchers could keep them for themselves if they wanted. They would be free to take those ghosts home, if they so wished, and to put them in their bedrooms or take them to school to show their friends.

"So," Mr. Copperstone said, "are we in agreement?"

It seemed that they were.

"When do we start?" Tim said.

"Immediately, if you want to," Mr. Copperstone said.

"But it's Monday," Tim pointed out. "And I'm being employed as a Weekend Boy. A Weekend Boy's not a Monday Boy, is he? There's a bit of a difference there."

"True, but time is—"

"Of the essence," Mr. Gibbings said.

"Indeed," Mr. Copperstone agreed. "And for that reason, should either or both of you wish to do a little ghost trapping work for an hour or so after school, we'll be happy to pay for it. The sooner you get started, the better—at least from our point of view. We can let you both have front door keys, so you may come and go as you wish."

Tim and Thruppence looked at each other. They both nodded.

"Okay," Thruppence said. "We'll do that."

"Just keep a record of the hours you've worked, and we'll pay you for them."

"Okay. That's a deal," Tim said.

"So when can you start?" Mr. Copperstone said. "I don't suppose . . . today?"

Tim shook his head. "Sorry. Too much homework."

"Far too much," Thruppence agreed.

"Then maybe tomorrow?"

Thruppence looked at Tim. "Tomorrow?"

"I could fit a bit of time in tomorrow," he said.

"Tomorrow it is then," Mr. Copperstone said, delighted. "Tomorrow it is. And who knows, by this time next week, we may have ourselves a ghost. Oh yes. We may have ourselves one very much alive and kicking ghost to show to our Mr. Beeston."

"I don't know so much about the alive and kicking part, Mr. Copperstone," Mrs. Scant said.

"No. True. Dead and kicking would do," Mr. Copperstone said. "Or not even kicking. Just as long as it's a ghost. Yes. Just one little ghost. That's all we need. Can you do that for us, do you think?"

"No problem," Tim said.

"We can do it if anyone can," Thruppence said. "Well, *I* can."

"And me, too."

"You can rely on us," Thruppence said. "Well, on me, anyway. I won't let you down. I don't know about him."

"Neither will I," Tim said emphatically. "So do we need a contract in writing for these jobs?"

"If our word is good enough for you, young man, then your word is good enough for us."

"Fine by me," Tim said.

"And me," Thruppence said.

"Then we shall look forward to seeing you tomorrow. And to a long—though not too long—and fruitful association."

"See you tomorrow, then," Thruppence said.

"Tomorrow it is," Tim agreed.

"By the way," Thruppence said, "I'll tell you one thing I'm going to do tomorrow before we get started on this ghost stuff."

"What is that, young lady?"

"I'm going to polish up your brass nameplate outside. It's a disgrace. You've let things slide there, you have."

"Yes, we have been remiss. We used to have a maintenance man to do it, but he retired and was never replaced," Mr. Copperstone explained.

"Well," Thruppence said, "how do you ever expect anyone to know you're here when they can't even see your nameplate? No wonder the ghosts aren't turning up. They probably don't know where to go. I'll bring my own buffer and polish. But I'll expect to be reimbursed."

"Of course, of course," Mr. Copperstone said.

Thruppence left it at that. Then she and Tim both left the Ministry and made their ways home.

"Like a breath of fresh air in the old place," Mr. Copperstone said once they had left. "The very presence of these youngsters just seems to blow the cobwebs away."

"Don't know why we didn't think of it years ago," Mrs. Scant said.

"Yes. Why didn't we?" Mr. Copperstone asked.

"Don't know," Mrs. Scant said.

"Anyway, back to work, I suppose, until five thirty. Though there isn't very long to go. Any chance of a cup of tea, Mrs. Scant?"

"Of course, sir. I'll go and boil the kettle."

And off she went to do so.

But she must have got distracted, for, as usual, the tea never arrived.

13
NO HUGS

Thruppence Coddley must have polished up the brass nameplate on her way to school early the next morning. For the sunlight now sparkled brightly off of it and it gleamed boldly with all the sharpness of new pins.

THE MINISTRY OF GHOSTS, the plate now proclaimed. Whereas previously the name had not so much proclaimed itself as shamefully muttered its existence with dull, smudged, shabby, and tarnished embarrassment.

A small wooden box had been left adjacent to the doorstep, and on this box Thruppence must have perched to enable her to reach the sign. She no doubt intended to retrieve the box on her way home that afternoon.

Under the box were two cloths—one for applying and one for buffing—and a bottle marked BEST FISH OIL POLISH. Not that there was any lingering smell of fish, just the faint aroma of strawberries.

Mr. Copperstone was the first to see the renovated sign.

Well, look at that now, he thought to himself. *See how it sparkles. It makes you proud to be in the Ministry. It real-*

ly does. Why, in some ways, it's just like the old days again. Back when we were busy and at the center of things. With comings and goings and the phone always ringing, and the telegram boy ever at the door with news of fresh ghost sightings or with requests from film stars to come and visit for an hour or two.

Truly, the Ministry of Ghosts had once been a lively and hectic place. The newspapers had written about it. Its progress was reported—on at least a weekly, if not a daily, basis.

MINISTRY ON VERGE OF NEW FIND!

FRESH EVIDENCE FOR EXISTENCE OF GHOSTS! PHOTOGRAPHS EXPECTED SOON! INTERVIEW WITH THE HEAD OF THE MINISTRY OF GHOSTS—EXCLUSIVE!

GHOSTS—SOON EVERY HOME WILL HAVE ONE, PROMISES MINISTER.

UNIONS THREATEN INDUSTRIAL ACTION UNLESS MINISTER GUARANTEES GHOSTS FOR THE WORKING MAN. ALL WE WANT IS EQUALITY, SPOKESMAN SAYS.

FEMINIST ORGANIZATION DEMANDS GHOSTS FOR WOMEN. DEMONSTRATION EXPECTED IN TRAFALGAR SQUARE.

ALLEGED MURDERER CLAIMS, "IT WAS A GHOST THAT DID IT!"

But when the ghosts did not appear, and when conclusive evidence never came, attention waned. The newspapers found other things to write about and the world moved on. Ghosts were a nine days' wonder, a fashion, a fad. The Ministry became a subject of ridicule.

WILL THE MINISTRY OF SPOOKS EVER FIND ONE? NOT A GHOST OF A CHANCE!

MINISTRY OF GHOSTS? OR MONEY DOWN THE DRAIN?

MINISTRY OF TIME-WASTERS. WHAT DO THESE CIVIL SERVANTS DO ALL DAY?

SPIRITS? THEY COULDN'T EVEN FIND SPIRITS IN A WHISKY DISTILLERY.

Then after ridicule, obscurity. The Ministry slipped from public view, sinking like a wrecked ship beneath the waters of the ocean, to lie on the deep, dark seabed out of sight and out of mind.

But now here was evidence of revival—a shimmering, sparkling brass plate.

• • •

At around eleven o'clock that morning, another exceptional event occurred in the Ministry of Ghosts: the telephone rang—with a real caller at the other end of it, not merely a salesman or a wrong number.

Mr. Copperstone stared at the phone—not that it was his job to immediately answer it. It was up to one of the staff to do that, and then, if necessary, to pass the call on to him. But he did wonder who was calling.

Is it, he thought, *for me?*

Downstairs the telephone simultaneously rang at the small switchboard by Mrs. Scant's desk.

In their adjacent offices, Mr. Gibbings and Miss Rolly looked up from their work; they stood and went to peer out into the hall.

"The telephone?" Miss Rolly said.

"Ringing?" Mr. Gibbings said. "At this time?"

"What am I to do, do you think?" Mrs. Scant said.

"Answer it!" Miss Rolly said decisively.

"You think I should?"

"Definitely!" Miss Rolly said.

"But cautiously, too," Mr. Gibbings counseled. "Nothing too abrupt."

Mrs. Scant darted back into her office.

"Hello," she was heard to say. "Ministry of Ghosts. How can I help you today?" Her voice took on a tremulous note. "Yes, sir. Yes, Mr. Beeston. He is. I'll put you through."

Then she was talking to Mr. Copperstone, saying, "Call for you, sir. It's that awful Mr. Beeston on the other line."

As much as Mr. Copperstone would have preferred not to talk to him, he was duty-bound to say, "Thank you, Mrs. Scant. Please put him through."

After a series of clicks, Beeston's voice boomed through the speakerphone on Mr. Copperstone's desk.

"Copperbum! Is that you?"

"Copperstone, actually, Mr. Beeston. And yes, it is me."

"Good. Now see here, Copplebum—"

"Stone!"

"See here, Stonebum, I'm ringing to see if there has been any progress. On the ghost front. You got one for me?"

"No, not yet. But you were only here last week and we do have three months, I believe . . ."

"Two months and three weeks now."

"Yes, well, we are working hard—"

"That'll make a nice change for you."

"As a matter of fact, we have engaged two freelance ghost hunters to—"

"Are they experienced?"

"Oh—enormously."

"How are you paying them?"

"We have the money all budgeted for."

"Well, you're not getting any extra. So don't think you are."

"We are quite confident, Mr. Beeston, that if anyone can find us a ghost, these two will be able to do it."

"What makes you think that?"

"Intuition," Mr. Copperstone said.

Beeston snorted derisively. "Intuition? Really? Well, I'll be calling again for further progress reports, so don't go thinking I've forgotten about you."

"No—"

"And you might care to mention to your staff that I've checked out the Ministry of Sewage and there is no shortage of vacancies. In fact, there's a nice sewage works about five miles down the river from you. I'm sure they'll fit in there nicely. So, good day to you then, Bubblewrap."

"Copperstone!"

"I'll be in touch."

At that, the line fell silent.

"Ignoramus," Mr. Copperstone muttered to himself. "All the manners of a warthog. The caliber of people in the service these days. They're just not gentlemen any-more."

He looked up from his desk and mutterings to find three faces peering at him around the door.

"Anything important, sir?" Mr. Gibbings asked.

"Just that Beeston fellow," Mr. Copperstone said. "Checking up on us. We've got two months and three weeks left to find a ghost."

It was frightening how the days sped away. It really was. Time just vanished like an apparition. It was here one moment, right in front of you, then suddenly it was gone, and you wondered if it had ever really been there at all.

• • •

That afternoon, once school was over, Thruppence Coddley and Tim Legge walked together down Bric-a-Brac Street in what might best be described as uneasy companionship.

They had never been enemies and yet, although they did not live far away from each other and were in the same class, they had never exactly been friends, either.

Tim had his crowd and Thruppence had hers, and so it was. There was the occasional nod, the intermittent, "Okay, then?" But little more than that. So the atmosphere between them was a bit uneasy.

It was Thruppence who decided to take the initiative.

"Tim," she said.

"What?" he said.

"I know you're not my best friend and I'm not yours, but I think that what we have to establish here is a professional working relationship."

"Fine by me," Tim said.

"We have to work together to find a ghost, but that doesn't mean we have to be all over each other and all lovey-dovey and stuff."

"Exactly," Tim said. "Just what I was thinking. I'm not into lovey-dovey."

"Nor me," Thruppence said.

"Especially not with girls," Tim said.

"Nor me, either," Thruppence said.

"Nor with boys, either, come to think of it," Tim said.

"Nor me," Thruppence said.

"In fact, I'm not the lovey-dovey type at all. Period. So we'll just keep things on a professional level, if you don't mind."

"Just what I was proposing," Thruppence said.

"Then let's shake on it," Tim said. "But no hugging. And no cuddles."

"Wouldn't dream of it," Thruppence said.

So they shook on the deal and agreed that they would work together as detached professionals to find a ghost. And while they agreed to look out for and to help each other—also on a professional basis—and to assist each other should either of them fall into danger, there was to be no lovey-dovey stuff and absolutely no hugging of any kind whatsoever. Unless hugging was needed, as in—for example—getting your arms around someone to pull them out of a barrel.

"Though I can't see either of us being stuck in a barrel," Tim said.

"Me neither," Thruppence said. "Though there is the possibility of someone getting stuck in a big drainpipe, perhaps."

"We'll just have to take it as it comes and play it by ear," Tim said.

"Exactly," Thruppence said. "And one more thing that I'd better make clear now is that just because my dad runs a fish shop, that doesn't mean I ever smell of herring. All I ever smell of is fresh strawberries. And if anyone ever says otherwise, there'll be trouble."

"Fair enough," Tim said. "Fine by me."

They had now arrived at the Ministry of Ghosts.

"Whoa, that nameplate's a bit bright now. What happened?"

"I polished it up this morning," Thruppence said. "Looks good, doesn't it? Dazzling, even."

"So, shall we knock on the knocker or . . . ?"

"They did give us a door key each and said come and go as you please . . ."

"All right," Tim said, fishing his key out from his pocket. He had attached it to his key ring, along with the keys for his house. "Let's go in."

"Hello!"

But there was no answer.

"They must be out," Tim said. "Or in a meeting."

"Maybe they're taking forty winks."

But there were no sounds of snoring either.

"Maybe they've gone home early?" Thruppence said.

"Yes. Maybe they just work a half day on Tuesdays."

"Hello!" Thruppence called again, but all she got in reply was a faint meow from somewhere.

"At least the cat's here somewhere."

"Well, it doesn't matter if they're here or not, for the moment," Thruppence said. "Come on, let's go and find the library. We can look at that book they were talking about."

"Grimes and Natterly's *Manual of Ghost Hunting*?"

"That's it. Come on."

They made their way past the grandfather clock. As they did the chimes struck the quarter hour with grim solemnity, even with foreboding.

"I couldn't live with that," Thruppence said. "Chiming away every quarter of an hour. Would drive me nuts."

They pushed open the door to the library and went inside. Grimes and Natterly's *Manual of Ghost Hunting* was not hard to find; it was lying on a table. And on the shelves around the room were hundreds, even thousands, of other books, all on ghosts and apparitions and the dead and the undead and the afterlife and the spirit world.

Tim picked one at random. Dust exploded from its pages, making him cough.

"We can't read all these," he said. "It would take years."

"Look at this one," Thruppence said. "*Ghosts and How to Exorcise Them.*"

"Exercise them?" Tim said.

"No, exorcise. Exorcise means to get rid of them."

"And how do you do that?"

"Bell, book, and candle, it says here."

"Oh," Tim said. "Is that right? Why can't you just tell them to go away?"

"They don't take any notice of you, I expect. Anyway, let's have a look in the index."

Thruppence turned to the back of Grimes and Natterly's *Manual of Ghost Hunting* and ran her finger down the index page until she came to C for Children.

"Here we are," she said. "There are about ten references here. There's 'Children: Attraction of Ghosts to.' And there's 'Children: as Bait to Lure Ghosts.' Then there's 'Children: Ghosts of.'"

"No thanks," Tim said. "We'll skip that."

"Then there's 'Children: Terrorizing of by Ghosts.'"

"Skip that, too."

"Hang on, look at this, though," Thruppence said. "Farther up at the top of the page. Look at this entry: 'Catching and Keeping Ghosts Once Found. How to Trap Ghosts and Stop Them from Escaping.'"

"Look it up," Tim said. "We're going to need to know that. Finding a ghost is only half of it. We've got to keep the ghost as well, to show people. Or how can we prove we've done our job?"

Thruppence leafed through the pages of the tome. It was a huge book, as thick as a monument and as wide as a flagstone, and when you turned a page over, it fluttered down like the wing of an eagle.

"Here we are."

"What's it say?"

They both read as follows:

It is essential, for the trapping of ghosts, to use a strong and robust glass container. No other material will do. Ghosts may pass through wood, through stonework, through iron and steel and solid walls. But they cannot pass through glass. Hence genies are kept in bottles—though a glass stopper must always be used. Never make the mistake of using a cork. If you try to use a cork, your ghost or genie will be out of the bottle immediately. Your ghost will disappear, and your genie will be up to untold mischief, as you are now no longer the master of it. A glass stopper is essential or a ghost catcher may come to a sticky end.

"A sticky end?" Tim said. "What does that mean?"

"You know," Thruppence said, "an end. That's sticky."

"But what sort of sticky?"

"Not very nice sticky, I would imagine."

"Hmm."

"But we should be all right on that front. I noticed plenty of glass jars and bottles in the storage room."

"Me, too."

"And they all seemed to have glass stoppers to them."

"Good."

"You know, those hinged ones on springs, like you get on soda bottles sometimes. Plus some screw tops."

"I know. Okay. So we know what to trap a ghost in. But how do we get it to go in there?"

"Hmm," Thruppence said. "That could be a problem."

"I mean," Tim said, "you can't just say, 'Excuse me, Mr. Ghost . . .'"

"Or Mrs. Ghost. Or Miss Ghost."

"Yes, all right, Thruppence. Or Miss Ghost."

"Or Ms. Ghost."

"Yes, all right."

"Or Dr. Ghost . . . Professor Ghost . . . Bishop Ghost—"

"Thruppence!"

"Sorry. Continue."

"Anyway, what I'm saying is you can't just expect a ghost to climb into a bottle because you want it to. It needs an incentive. Some motivation. Something to get it in there."

"Let's look it up."

Thruppence turned back to the index and found what looked like an appropriate entry.

"Bottle. Persuading Ghost to Go Into. Suggested Methods. Page three-seven-one," she read out.

She turned to it.

It is one thing to lure your ghost to appear before you. To bottle it is another. There are tried and tested methods for the bottling of ghosts. But none can be guaranteed. The temperaments of ghosts are as varied and variable as those of the living. Ghosts are individuals, and what works for one ghost will not work for another. In all things the ghost hunter must be alert and adaptable.

Suggestions for entrapment of ghosts in bottles:
1) Place something into the bottle relating to the ghost's past. A small picture from a locket. An item of jewelry. A fragment of a once loved thing. NB: The problem with this method is that the ghost catcher may know nothing of the ghost's past or possess no such personal items.
2) Place something into the bottle of an enticing nature. A bon-bon, perhaps. A gold coin.
3) Place something into the bottle to excite the ghost's curiosity. A folded note, for example, with something written on it. A rare and unusual item. A novelty of some sort, a puzzle, a knickknack, a toy.
4) Some ghosts may be lured into a container by a burning candle—but, caution, the candle will not burn long for lack of air, and the heat may explode the glass.
5) Many ghosts may be seduced by scents and perfumes. Dried flowers, for example. Tinctures and essences and exotic oils. They are particularly fond of the smell of roses and even more so of the scent of fresh strawberries.

"Fresh strawberries . . ."

It was Tim who spoke. Thruppence raised her eyes and looked into his. Neither of them said anything else. Yet they both suddenly felt very alone in that seemingly deserted building. Just them and the books and the silence and the motes of dust forever floating in the shafts of sunlight that intermittently broke the gloom.

Thruppence cleared her throat.

"Yes," she said. "Well, we've got a few ideas then. We'll just have to try things out as we go along and see what happens."

"Exactly," Tim said. "That's what we'll do. So, what about step one?"

"Step one?"

"Yes," Tim said. "We've got an idea of how to trap the ghost—which has to be step two. But how do we get it to appear in the first place—step one?"

"Maybe we'd better leave that until tomorrow," Thruppence said. "I have to get home or my parents will wonder where I am."

But when she looked at her watch, instead of an hour having passed, as she had imagined, only fifteen minutes had gone by.

"We can stay a little longer, can't we?" Tim said.

"Okay. But I'll tell you what—is it me or do you think it's a bit spooky in here?"

"Well, I guess it would have to be," Tim said. "It is the Ministry of Ghosts, after all."

"I suppose," Thruppence said. "But don't forget, even if things do get really spooky at any point along the way here . . . just remember—no hugs."

"No hugs," Tim agreed. "Absolutely not." With that, he reached for another book.

Softly, softly, catchee monkey, Tim thought to himself as he turned the pages. And maybe it was the same for ghostees, too.

14
PLANS

It was quite cool, Tim Legge felt, to have your own key to the front door of the Ministry of Ghosts.

How many boys his age had a privilege and a responsibility like that? He slept with the key under his pillow. But he told his parents nothing about it. He had a feeling, possibly a justified one, that they would not understand.

Either they would say, "Tim, it's all nonsense!" or they would say, "Tim, there are things beyond our knowledge in this world—dangerous things—and you shouldn't go messing around with them."

Or they might say, "Tim, what do you mean you've got a weekend job? And not only that, it sounds like a Monday, Tuesday, Wednesday, Thursday, and Friday nights' job, too. It'll interfere with your homework. You'll get too tired and break out with boils. We forbid you to do it!"

And he didn't want to lose his job. Not when he had a birthday coming up every year and a present to buy for himself.

• • •

A few streets away, staring up at the ceiling of her own bedroom, Thruppence Coddley was having similar thoughts. It felt good to be entrusted with major responsibilities, both somewhat scary and rather exciting. It felt good to have the key to the Ministry of Ghosts under her pillow. But it wasn't the sort of thing to mention to her parents.

"If you want a weekend job, Thruppence, you can help out with the fish."

No. She was happy to help with her dad's paperwork, but she didn't want to deal with fish. She'd done enough of that already. Fish were no good to a girl who only ever smelled of strawberries. And fresh ones, at that.

There were other problems, too.

Thruppence was sure she had once heard her father say that children under a certain age could not do any kind of paid work at all. You had to be at least thirteen to work a paper route. She was sure that was true.

But they didn't seem bothered about things like that at the Ministry. Not old, kindly Mr. Copperstone or fierce but friendly Miss Rolly or nice but shy Mr. Gibbings or eccentric Mrs. Scant with her endless promises of tea that never arrived.

They were a funny bunch all right. Tucked away there in their offices, out of sight and out of mind, with their tarnished brass plate—well, shiny now, thanks to Thruppence—and their old-world ways and with their out-of-style clothes and old-fashioned manners.

They didn't seem to know what was going on, really. They seemed out of touch with the modern world. Mrs.

Scant still had that battered old typewriter on her desk, an immense thing almost the size of a washing machine, Thruppence reckoned. They really needed to get a few laptops in there and to bring themselves up to speed.

Thruppence's eyes began to close. The key under her pillow felt as if it were emanating warmth. For a moment she imagined she could hear—even feel—a heartbeat, as if the key were a living thing.

But all this was in her imagination, of course. And as she sank into sleep, her mind dwelt on the problem of where and how to catch a ghost.

"I'll sleep on it," Thruppence told herself, as her wakefulness turned to drowsiness, and as her thoughts turned to dreams.

"Sleep on it . . . and then in the morning . . . I'll have the answer. Yes. I'll have the answer . . . in the mor . . ."

Then she was fast asleep.

When morning came, she was woken by the sound of voices and clattering wooden boxes. Out in the yard the truck had come with supplies of fresh fish, with lobsters from Cornwall and herring from Scotland and salmon from the same place and whelks and prawns from who knew where.

Suddenly, she had the solution.

She and Tim Legge had the apparatus, and they had the means to trap a ghost. All they needed was the place where they'd find a ghost—and Thruppence knew just the spot.

• • •

Back at the head office, the granite-faced Mr. Beeston pressed a buzzer on his desk to summon his assistant, Mrs. Peeve.

She came promptly (if not all that willingly, as she had been interrupted while eating a snack) and asked what she could do.

Mr. Beeston had a file open upon his desk.

"It's this Ministry again, Mrs. Peeve," he said. "This obscure department of ours, this Ministry of Ghosts, which no one seems to know much about, and which seems to have slipped down the back of a filing cabinet for the last twenty years."

"Yes, sir. And . . . what is your concern with it now?"

"Well, I went to see them, as you know, and I set them straight, Mrs. Peeve."

"Did you, sir?"

"Very much so, Mrs. Peeve. I set them straight big time. And I think you'll agree that when it comes to setting people straight—"

"Absolutely, sir."

"I set them so straight they're vertical. I told them to get to work, too. And I think you'll also agree, Mrs. Peeve, that when it comes to telling people to get to work—"

"You are one of our most experienced operatives in that field, Mr. Beeston, without question."

"I gave them an ultimatum. I said, find a ghost in three months' time—a proper, all-singing, all-dancing ghost that we can all see for ourselves and get a good look at—or this Ministry of yours is going to be closed down."

"Yes, sir."

"Quaking in their boots, they were, Mrs. Peeve."

"Yes, sir."

"However, I've been looking at the files here, and I can't seem to find any detailed records for the staff or their employment history. Nothing about academic qualifications, dates of birth, when first hired, and so forth. It's just general documents here. But where's the specifics?"

"Their personal details ought to be there, sir."

"Ought to be is not the same as actually is, though, is it, Mrs. Peeve?"

"No, sir."

"So kindly get yourself over to the Human Resources Office, Mrs. Peeve, have a good look, and get a hold of the personnel records for these four names: Copperstone, Gibbings, Scant, and Rolly."

"Yes, sir."

"I want to find out what these four have been up to; where they come from; and what they did before they got these cushy little jobs for themselves at the Ministry of Spooks."

"Ghosts, to give it its official title, sir."

"Spooks, ghosts, same difference. Just get the records, if you can. I want to know how old that Copperstone is and whether I can actually make him retire. And I want to see whether the other three are suitable material for the Sewage Department."

"I'm sure they would be, sir."

"We'll have to see about that. It's not just anyone who can work in sewage. You need a flair for it. We have to make sure, Mrs. Peeve, that public sewage is in the right hands."

"Yes, sir."

"Well, continue on, Mrs. Peeve."

"I'll continue on, sir."

Mr. Beeston handed her the file; she took it and left the room. Mr. Beeston walked to the window, looked out over the busy city street, stretched, yawned, returned to his desk, and grabbed another file from his inbox.

He folded back the Manila cover and glanced at the page in front of him.

THE MINISTRY OF DUCKS, the title page read.

"Ministry of Ducks," Mr. Beeston muttered. "This sounds like another one. This sounds like another load of dead wood we'll be able to get rid of. What do we need a Ministry of Ducks for? I'll have to pay them a visit."

• • •

"Where?" Tim Legge said. "The what?"

They were in a confidential corner of the playground, where Thruppence Coddley had dragged him, though he would rather have been kicking a ball around with his friends.

"The cemetery," she said. "The graveyard."

"The graveyard! Why do we want to go hanging around graveyards?" Tim said. "Not very lively there, is it?"

"Because that's where we'll stand a good chance of catching a ghost."

He looked at her. "How do you know?"

"Because that's where the dead bodies are, of course," Thruppence said. "It stands to reason. Dead bodies—ghosts. You know, walking the midnight hour and all that."

"Walking the midnight hour? You mean we'd have to go there at midnight?"

"Well, ghosts are hardly going to show up during the day, are they? Not in broad daylight. And even if they did, how would you see them in bright sunlight? You couldn't."

"Well . . ." Tim said. "I don't know . . ."

"Unless you're scared, of course."

"Scared!" Tim said indignantly. "Me? Scared? I'm not scared. I've spent lots of nights in cemeteries, lots of them. I used to sneak out and go down there all the time. Me and my friend Steve—we'd go there and have picnics and late-night feasts. We'd sit there on a tombstone with a bottle of soda and a bag of chips. Done that many times, I have."

"Then it won't bother you to do it once more, will it?"

"Um . . . no."

"So, what about tonight?"

"Tonight! Isn't that a bit, well, sudden?"

"Strike while the iron's hot," Thruppence said.

"What iron?"

"No time like the present," she said.

"You know it's my birthday soon," Tim said, "speaking of presents . . ."

"So, are you coming or not? Or do I have to do it on my own? Which means I'll get the bonus on my own and keep it all for me."

"Hang on. Who said I wasn't coming? I didn't say . . . the only thing is, Thruppence, how do we catch it?"

"We'll pick up one of those thick glass jars with the big glass stoppers on our way home. We'll get it from the Ministry."

"And how do we get the ghosts to show up? What if there aren't any hanging around the cemetery? What if they've—I don't know—gone off on a vacation or something?"

"Then we have to think again. But I noticed there's a section in that book—"

"Grimes and Natterly's *Manual of Ghost Hunting*?"

"That's it. And it tells you how to summon ghosts with incantations."

"What are those?"

"Chants and special words and ritual sayings and stuff. And we need a candle and some drops of water and—"

"I hope we don't need any eye of newt," Tim said. "Have you heard of that? Eye of newt? They're always going on in books about eye of newt when it comes to ghosts and things. But I haven't a clue where you'd get any eye of newt from. Maybe I could get a bit of frogspawn or some bird droppings, but as for eye of newt—"

"We don't need any eye of newt," Thruppence snapped, her patience wearing thin. She began to think that maybe Tim Legge was not the ideal ghost-hunting partner, at least not the kind she would have wished for, and that as a Weekend Boy, he was dead weight.

"It says in the book that we just need something alluring," she continued. "Something fragrant or pungent to remind the ghost of its past life and to tempt it in. It also says a lot of ghosts have unfinished business."

"I've heard of that—unfinished business," Tim said. "It's a bit like un-started homework, isn't it?"

"No, it isn't," Thruppence said. "It's when ghosts have things on their minds from when they were alive and they want to come back to fix them and to put things right. Like to search for justice. Or to apologize for bad behavior they may now regret. And they can't move on until they've done this. And that's why they're ghosts, trapped on the earth, and why they can't move on to other dimensions."

"How do you know all this?" Tim demanded.

"I read the flipping book!" Thruppence said. "The one we had in front of us yesterday. You were sitting right next to me. What were you doing?"

"I was looking at the pictures," Tim said. "Did you see that drawing of the ghost with his head under his arm and his ear in his back pocket?"

The whistle blew for the end of recess.

"Look, we can't talk any more about it now. Are you up for tonight or not? Can you sneak out of bed and meet me at the cemetery at midnight or can't you?"

"I think so," Tim said, not wishing to appear like a wimp. "That won't be a problem."

"Okay. We'll need the equipment first and all the gear. And we'll need to write down the incantations. I don't think they'll let us take the ghost-hunting manual with us. It would be far too heavy anyway. I'll see you outside the Ministry after school this afternoon."

"All right. I'll see you there."

"Don't be late," Thruppence told him. They went back to their class.

Cemetery, Tim thought. *Midnight. Ghosts. Dead people*. What if there are zombies, too? Or vampires? Or werewolves? Or badgers?

It was a scary prospect. But he wasn't going to chicken out. (There wouldn't be chickens, would there?)

No. It might be scary, but he'd do it. Tim Legge was only human, and human beings feel fear, but he would persevere and overcome it.

Tim Legge would be there. You could depend on that.

15
A VISIT TO THE CEMETERY

They knocked first, wondering if anyone would be there or if they would all have gone home early, as they had yesterday.

But the staff was in, and the front door creaked open to reveal Mrs. Scant, who smiled at the two young visitors.

"Oh, our Weekend help!" she said. "Do come inside."

They went in and the door, which seemed to have a propensity to close of its own accord, clicked shut behind them.

"Is it Mr. Copperstone you want to see?" Mrs. Scant asked. "Because—to be honest—I suspect he may be napping. But I can easily—"

"No, please don't disturb him, Mrs. Scant," Thruppence said. "We just need to get some ghost-hunting stuff from the storage room and to make a few notes from the manual."

"Oh, then go straight downstairs and help yourselves," Mrs. Scant said. "You know the way. And will you be wanting a cup of tea . . . ?"

But both Thruppence and Tim knew that even if they had answered yes, their chances of ever getting any tea were slim. So they declined and said they would continue with the matters at hand.

On their way to the storage room, they passed Mr. Gibbings's and Miss Rolly's offices.

Hearing their footsteps, Mr. Gibbings, whose door was open, pretended not to be working on the crossword that lay in front of him on his desk, and he did his best to look busy—mostly by means of frowns and grimaces, none of which were convincing.

"Hello," he waved. "Can't chat, I'm afraid. Up to here in work." And he indicated his chin as a measure of the depth and height of his labor.

They passed Miss Rolly's office. Her door was slightly ajar. She didn't hear them. She was intently reading a book propped up in front of her. Its title was: *Women's Suffrage: The Battle for the Vote*.

Waiting to be read when that volume was finished was another tome, entitled: *Equal Wages, Equal Rights*.

• • •

Things in the storage room were just as Tim and Thruppence had left them the day before. While Thruppence wrote down the necessary words and incantations for the raising of ghosts from Grimes and Natterly's *Manual of Ghost Hunting*, Tim selected a heavy glass vessel with a large glass stopper. He made sure that the one fit the other and that there was a good seal between them.

Not going to get out of there in a hurry, he thought.

He stuffed the glass jar and stopper into his backpack. Together they seemed to weigh a ton.

"How are you getting along?" he asked Thruppence, who was busy with pen and notebook.

"I've nearly finished," she said. "Almost got it all down."

"You know," Tim said, "I was thinking about bait. Ghost bait."

"Ghost bait?"

"To put in the jar to lure it in. Something pungent."

"Yes?"

"I thought maybe . . . how about . . . one of your dad's herrings?"

Thruppence put down her pen.

"Herring?"

"Yeah, a herring. You get one of your dad's herrings, and we'll put it in the jar. And if you bring one of your dad's herrings to lure the ghost in, then I could maybe bring one of my dad's old wooden legs along— there's a few in the basement, left over from the old days. Then, if there's trouble, we can bash the ghost over the head."

"With a wooden leg?"

"What do you think?" Tim said.

"Tim," Thruppence said, "a ghost is a spirit, isn't it? It isn't solid. So how can you hit it over the head with a wooden leg? The wooden leg'll go straight through it."

"You're splitting hairs a bit," Tim said.

"No, I'm not."

"We could still use it for knocking the stopper into the glass container. And also for defending ourselves, like if instead of summoning a ghost we accidentally get a zombie by mistake."

"A zombie?"

"Yeah. They're pretty solid, aren't they? Or a were-wolf. Be very handy to have a wooden leg in your hand if a werewolf attacked you."

"Tim—"

"No harm in being careful . . ."

Thruppence stared at him, open-mouthed. There were many thoughts going through her mind and many things she could have said, but she decided against saying most of them. Instead, what she said was, "Tim, why do you think a herring is going to lure a ghost?"

"It might have been fond of herring while it was alive."

There was, undeniably, a kind of logic and reason to this. But Thruppence still felt that it was unlikely.

"Don't you think something a bit more, well—a nicer smell might be better?"

"I'm prepared," Tim said, "to give a herring a go. I mean, if you want to catch a mouse, you use a bit of cheese; a fish—a worm. If you want to catch a spider, you use a fly. If you want to catch a ghost, what's wrong with trying a herring?"

Thruppence sighed.

"All right, Tim," she said. "I have to say that I think this is kind of a long shot. But I guess we're doing this job together. So, if you want to try a herring to start with, then I'll bring one along."

"If it doesn't work, we can maybe try a cookie," Tim said.

Thruppence completed her notes.

"Do you have the jar?" she said.

"In my bag."

"All right. Come on."

Mr. Gibbings was still doing his crossword and Miss Rolly reading her books. Neither looked up as the two children went past. At the front door they called out their goodbyes and a "See ya later!" came from Mrs. Scant. Mr. Copperstone was, presumably, still at his afternoon slumber. He would wake up just before it was time to go home, his day's work over, and then he could enjoy a well-deserved rest.

• • •

The old grandfather clock in the corridor of the Ministry of Ghosts chimed its longest chime. It did so twice a day to mark the end of the old day and the start of the new, and also at the halfway point in between.

On this occasion, the chimes rang at midnight, and they echoed eerily, not merely through the building but out onto the deserted cobbles of Bric-a-Brac Street. Somewhere a cat meowed and a rival responded, and then there was a scattering of milk bottles, and then the chimes fell silent and midnight was here. Midnight, the witching hour, when (according to those who believed in such things) ghosts walked the earth.

A door creaked half a mile away. A back door. A back door belonging to the fishmonger's shop, Good Coddley's, and out into the alleyway, all dressed in dark clothes and with soft shoes on her feet and with written-out spells in her pocket for the summoning up of ghosts, came Thruppence Coddley herself. In her hand she held a plastic pouch, tightly sealed, and inside that pouch was . . . a herring.

Treading lightly and with caution, Thruppence skirted around to the front of the shop, glancing up at the windows to ensure she had not been heard leaving and that all were still slumbering within. Then, the more distance she put between herself and home, the more her step grew jaunty, confident, and carefree. She hastened along the cobblestones in the direction of a dark spire a few streets away, silhouetted against a cloud-empty sky by the light of a roving moon. This was St. Bindle's Church, the local place of worship, and once (though no longer) of burial. Its ancient graveyard had long since been filled up, and the deceased now sought fresh pastures farther outside of town. The gravestones here were old and tumbling, with faded letters etched upon them and many unrecognizable names of those who had fallen asleep or were with their maker or who were enjoying peace at last.

Thruppence was approaching the graveyard from the south, heading in a northerly direction. Approaching from the west and heading in an easterly direction were other soft footsteps. Someone else was out at that hour. He, too, was stepping lightly, a procedure that was complicated in his case by the heavy contents of the backpack on his shoulder and by the weight of the large, adult-sized wooden leg under his arm.

This, of course, was Tim Legge. Unlike Thruppence, he had not snuck out of the back door, but had made his exit by the front. But he had been equally cautious in feigning sleep when his mother had looked in on him and had been every bit as silent in dressing, in turning the bedroom door handle, and in tiptoeing down the stairs. Now here he was, heading for the prearranged rendezvous with his fellow ghost hunter, where he hoped to meet not just her, but at least one—if not a larger quantity—of ghosts.

Thruppence was first to arrive. She selected the most comfortable looking of the gravestones and perched herself upon it. A yew tree grew among the graves; there were always yew trees in cemeteries, though she did not know why. The church spire above her pointed the way to heaven and showed her where the moon was and the sparkling stars, too.

There was a sound . . . but it didn't bother her. She knew who it was.

"Tim—is that you?"

"Yeah. Is that you?"

"Who else would it be? Did you get out all right?"

"No trouble. You?"

"Fine."

"Anyone see you?"

"No. At least I don't think so. You?"

"No. Did you bring your stuff?"

"Yes, here. Did you?"

"Yeah, here."

Tim brandished the wooden leg. Thruppence looked at it, somewhat nonplussed.

"Couldn't you have brought one of your cricket bats instead? Or one of the baseball bats your dad makes? They'd be a bit easier to use than this. I mean, if you want to whack someone over the head, a wooden leg isn't what you'd call ideal, is it?"

"My dad would miss one of his bats, but he won't miss one of his legs," Tim said.

"I'll have to take your word for that," Thruppence said. "And have you brought the big glass jar?"

"Here," Tim said, carefully opening his backpack and taking the glass vessel out. It was like a very big jam jar but with a thread in the inside of the neck, so that the equally heavy glass stopper could be screwed in tight. The glass of the jar was so thick you could barely see into it, and the glass, instead of clear, was a deep green-blue.

"Where's the herring?" he said. "You haven't forgotten it?"

Wordlessly, and with an attitude of some disdain, Thruppence held out the plastic bag and Tim took it from her. He peeled it open and pushed the herring into the jar. He had to force it a bit, but he finally got it inside then he shook the jar around so that the herring fell flat to the bottom.

"Looks tempting to me," Tim said. Then he looked around for a trash can. "What'll I do with this bag?"

"Over there."

He went and dropped it into the garbage.

"Okay," Tim said. "You got the spells then and the hallucinations?"

"Incantations!" Thruppence snapped.

"Incantations, hallucinations, same difference," Tim said.

"Nothing at all—"

They both heard a rustling in the long grass behind the gravestones.

"What was that?"

They froze. Waited. Stared. Silence again.

"Just the wind," Thruppence said.

"There isn't any," Tim pointed out.

"Maybe a cat, then. Or a hedgehog. Or a squirrel. Whatever it was, it's gone."

But it wasn't. It was a small urban fox, which poked its nose out from behind a gravestone, saw the two figures, appeared more startled by them than they did by it, and ran off as fast as all four legs would take it.

"See. Just a fox," Thruppence said. "So come on, let's get to work."

Each of them had brought a flashlight along, but they were not needed. The moonlight was bright enough to read the inscriptions on the stones—at least those not lost to erosion caused by wind and rain and weather.

"How about here?" Tim said. "There's hundreds of them in here."

While "hundreds" was something of an exaggeration, there were certainly more than one. He was standing by a small mausoleum in which several generations of the same family were interred. The family name was, somewhat appropriately, Stiff. Several Stiffs slumbered there together.

"We'll have more of a chance if there's a lot of them," Tim said. "I mean, one grave, well, the person in there might have been quite a happy person and have no reason for wanting to come back and . . . whatsit again?"

"Walk the earth," Thruppence said.

"Yeah. Walk the earth. But if you've got a big mob of them, well, there's bound to be a couple of discontents . . ."

"Maybe," Thruppence said.

"There's bound to be someone with unfinished business, doomed to . . . what was it again?"

"Walk the earth."

"Walk the earth. So I suggest we try here first. Let's get the Stiffs up."

"All right," Thruppence said. "Though I don't really see why we can't just use the incantations and the spell for the whole cemetery."

"We only want one ghost," Tim pointed out. "Not thousands of them. There won't be room in the jar. They'll suffocate in there—"

"Tim," Thruppence pointed out, "ghosts aren't going to suffocate. Ghosts are dead."

"Well, you know what I mean," Tim said. "We don't want overcrowding. It could be a health and safety issue."

Thruppence wasn't entirely sure that she did know what he meant. But never mind that for now, she told herself.

"Okay. Are you ready with the stopper to seal up the jar if a ghost does appear?" she asked.

"Ready as I'll ever be," Tim said.

"All right. Let's get busy."

Swiftly, but surely, following the copied-down instructions from Grimes and Natterly's *Manual of Ghost Hunting*, Thruppence got to work.

Taking a stick from the ground, she traced out a hexagon—a six-sided star shape—in the moss that overgrew the stone lid of the tomb. Next, Thruppence took a small candle from her backpack—a tea light that she had borrowed from the kitchen drawer—and she lit it by means of matches she had taken from the same place.

"Shouldn't really be using matches at your age," Tim said.

"I happen to be highly sensible," Thruppence told him. "And you're spoiling my concentration."

The night was so calm that the flame of the candle burned without a flicker. It cast a warm, ethereal glow. A cloud appeared in the sky above now and crossed the moon. Thruppence placed the candle in the middle of the hexagon.

"Okay," she said. "Here goes nothing. You ready?"

Tim nodded that he was ready. And indeed he looked ready—ready for anything.

At his feet was the jar with the herring inside—bait for any ghosts that might appear. In his hand was the stopper for the jar and as soon as a ghost was inside, he was ready to clamp that stopper into the hole at the top and to screw it tight. Not far away from him, well within snatching-up distance, leaning on a gravestone was the wooden leg. One whack with that and a man would be rendered unconscious. What it might do to a ghost, who knew? But there was no harm in trying.

The cloud sailed on like a lonely ship in an empty sea.

"Okay. Let's say the words—together."

Thruppence held up the paper with the incantation written upon it, and they both read the words out loud, their voices blending together, seeming to turn into one:

"I summon all ye ghosts and spirits,

All ye phantoms, all ye sprites,
All ye sad, unhappy creatures,
Doomed by fate to walk the night."

They paused; they waited; nothing yet, just the burning candle and the height of the spire and the stars and the moon and the quiet of night, and in the far, far distance a sound of perhaps a baby crying or a small animal, lamenting its hunger or its pain.

"I summon all ye wraiths and demons,
All ye specters, trapped in time,
And all ye fiends—for any fiend
Of yours is a fiend of mine."

Again they paused. Again they waited. The candle flickered now. The air felt cooler. There were signs of a faint mist laying on the ground, even rising from it, like cotton wool.

"I summon all ye apparitions,
Command that ye will now appear.
Make thy presence known and certain,
Make thy features sharp and clear."

Now a definite chill and a wide silence, so profound that they scarcely dared to break it and yet they had to go on to the final verse:

"Come to me without delay,
Come to me—thy crimes confess.
And with this book and with this candle,
I will help you to find rest."

It wasn't a book, strictly speaking, it was a piece of paper with things copied from a book on it. But Thruppence didn't feel that should matter. So the spell was done. All there was to do now was to wait.

The seconds stretched long and distant, seeming like hours. But then there were noises, whisperings, fleeting and remote at first but coming nearer—surely, coming nearer.

"Thruppence . . ."

"I hear it," she whispered back.

They stood, tense, at the ready, full of fear now, but fighting the fear with all their will.

Then footsteps came. But this was not—surely not—the approach of some wraith or spirit without material substance. This was . . . this was something else.

"Thruppence, what have we done? It's not a ghost . . . it sounds like . . ."

The steps continued, firm and solid, flat and sturdy, moving with a dull rhythm in some lifeless, mechanical way, as if the steps were those of a creature not from this world. They sounded like the steps of some zombie-like thing, a Frankenstein's monster, with horrible bolts in its neck, composed of the parts of fresh corpses stitched and fashioned together. The steps continued. Here it was now, coming from behind the yew tree and casting a huge, an immense, a giant towering shadow in the moonlight.

"Thruppence, I don't know what we've done, but that's no ghost. That's something else. That's something awful coming."

"I know. Grab your stuff. Come on. Let's get out of here!"

Tim didn't need to be told twice. He grabbed the things that were within reach. He snatched up the jar—

though the herring fell from it—and stuffed it into his backpack. The wooden leg he had to leave behind. In seconds he and Thruppence were leaping over grass and gravel, over grave and tombstone, and they were running with all the speed they could muster, and they didn't dare to look back once.

They only slowed for breath when they felt the familiar friendliness of cobblestones under their feet, and they found themselves—though they had not realized they had run so far—in Bric-a-Brac Street and right outside of the Ministry of Ghosts. But the place looked quiet and even friendly, far friendlier than what they had left behind. It was all in darkness, with only the moonlight upon its windows and the brass plate smiling by the door.

"You don't think it's coming after us, do you? Whatever it was. You don't think it saw us? You don't think it knows where we live?"

"No, I don't think so," Thruppence said. "I think we're safe now. Come on, let's get to the end of the road, then you go your way and I'll go mine—"

"We have to go home alone?"

"We can't go home together, Tim."

"Well, you can take me home first, and then—"

"I can't. But you'll be all right. It didn't see us. It probably just lives in the cemetery anyway and that's where it stays."

"But what was it? A zombie? A vampire?"

"I don't know, but I'll tell you one thing, I'm not going back to find out."

Tim realized that one of his belongings was missing.

"Thruppence," he said. "My wooden leg! I left it behind."

"Well, you're not going back for it, are you? Didn't you say your dad wouldn't miss it?"

"Hmm, I guess not."

"Then leave it; don't worry about it. Okay. I've got to go. I'll see you in the morning. We'll have to think of another plan."

"You're going to keep trying?"

"Of course," Thruppence said. "Aren't you?"

"Um . . . yeah, of course. If you are."

"If at first you don't succeed . . ."

"Yeah, all right. Well, I'm going to run home now. I'll see you tomorrow."

"Okay, Tim. See you tomorrow. And, Tim . . ."

"What?"

"Watch out for monsters."

Tim Legge did not reply. He just ran off down the road and did not stop until he was back at The Legge Works. Soon he was in bed and safely under the covers, his heart pounding and his nerves frayed, but he had survived; he had lived to tell the tale. And soon he was asleep.

Thruppence ran home, too. She was also soon in bed and her eyes were closing.

I wonder what it was, she thought, as she drifted into dreams. *I wonder what that creature was, to cast such a shadow and to have such heavy, plodding steps. Its breath sounded so awful, too—so guttural and harsh, like the breathing of some ghastly, horrible thing. But I suppose I'll never find out now. Never.*

Only Thruppence Coddley was wrong in her supposition. She would see the monster again. Oh yes. She would see it all too clearly.

It would visit her; it would come to her very home one day; it would stand on her very threshold and look down upon her from its height with its dark, piercing eyes.

But fortunately she did not know that.

And so, while she was still able to, she slept.

16
WHO? OR WHAT?

The terrors of the night often fade to nothing with the coming of the day. The sun seems to bleach and to diminish them. Giants shrink; monsters shrivel; zombies look like nothing more than ordinary commuters, bleary-eyed and a bit short of sleep.

What had terrified Tim Legge the night before did not frighten him so much the morning after. He awoke emboldened by the daylight and by the sun shining through the curtains.

It wasn't a zombie at all, he thought to himself. *It was probably just . . .*

He found himself a bit stuck though. If not a zombie, what had it been? It had been big and flat-footed and wide and bulky, and it had moved with slow but deliberate and unstoppable menace.

Maybe it was . . . a policeman, Tim thought. And the more he thought so, the more he convinced himself that was what it had been. *Yeah. It was a policeman who'd seen the candle glow and heard the incantations and stuff and so stopped by to investigate.*

That could be it. Yes. Of course it could. And it was just as well they had run away, even though it probably had just been a policeman. Because a policeman would have demanded an explanation.

"What's going on here?" he would have said. (Policemen always said that. Tim had seen it on TV.) "What are you two up to after midnight at the back of the church with a herring and a wooden leg?"

It would have been tricky to come up with a convincing explanation. The truth would certainly not have worked. You can't go telling policemen you're hunting for ghosts. There's probably a law against it.

"Do your parents know you're out this late?"

That would have been the next question. Then it really would have gotten complicated. So it had been a good thing that they had made a run for it.

But it couldn't really have been a monster—could it?

Tim got dressed and went downstairs for breakfast.

"Did you hear any bumping and banging late last night?" his mother asked him.

"No," Tim said. "Not a sound."

"Funny," she said. "Your dad and I thought we heard something. Like a door banging or something like that."

Tim left for school early. He had already made his mind up to return to the cemetery and see if he could retrieve the wooden leg. For Tim was not the kind of boy to turn his back on a perfectly good leg. He may have run away from his leg the night previously, but now he was coming back for it.

As he approached St. Bindle's Church, he spotted a figure already moving among the gravestones. He halted in his tracks. But then, seeing that the figure was about his own size and closely resembled Thruppence Coddley, he continued walking and entered the cemetery.

"Hey, Thruppence."

"I don't respond to 'hey,'" Thruppence said, looking up from a gravestone. "If you want to talk to me it's not 'Hey, Thruppence.' It's 'Hello Thruppence, how are you today?' That's far better."

"What are you looking for?" Tim said.

"My herring," Thruppence said. "I'm not the kind of girl to leave a herring behind. Or if I have to due to circumstances, I come back for it. I was worried a small animal might eat it and get a bone stuck in its throat."

"Well, I'm looking for my leg," Tim said.

"You're standing on it," Thruppence told him.

"The wooden one."

"Well, I can't see it anywhere. Or my herring either. I reckon that whoever has your leg has got my herring, too."

"That thing last night, you mean?" Tim said.

"Exactly," Thruppence said. "Only what *was* that thing last night?"

"Well, I've been thinking about that—" Tim began. But before he could elaborate, Thruppence interrupted.

"So have I," Thruppence said. "And you know what I think it was—"

"It was a policeman," Tim said.

"It was," Thruppence corrected him, "one of the undead."

All the fear and terror of the night before returned and with a vengeance. Tim felt his chest grow tight; his windpipe felt constricted.

"What do you mean . . . the undead? You mean it was what we were looking for . . . a ghost?"

"No," Thruppence said. "Ghosts are all right. That is, they can be trouble, but they're nothing compared to the living dead. Because you have to die to be a ghost. But the undead, well, they're neither one thing nor the other. They aren't dead, and they aren't alive either. They're just sort of half-and-half and slowly going moldy with the occasional part falling off—like a couple of fingers or a toe. And if they get you in their clammy embrace—"

"Clammy embrace?" Tim said. "I don't like the sound of that."

"No, you want to avoid all that if you can," Thruppence told him. "Because if they get you in their clammy embrace, they slowly squeeze half the life out of you, and you turn into one of the undead yourself."

Tim felt his hand clutching his throat, as if to reassure himself that he was still breathing.

"But I thought it was maybe . . . just a policeman."

"Policeman!" Thruppence sneered. "You have got an imagination, haven't you, Tim?"

"But where did it come from?"

"It probably lives around here somewhere."

"I thought you said it was one of the undead. So how can it *live* around here?"

"All right, it *dies* around here somewhere, if you're going to be picky. But it was the undead, if you ask me. You take my word for it. And look . . ."

Thruppence pointed down. There, in the soft earth of a flower bed, was a huge—no, an immense—footprint.

"What is that?" Tim said. "It has to be an elephant at the very least. I've never seen a footprint that big. Not outside of the zoo."

"That," Thruppence said, "has to have been left by the creature we saw last night. That," she said again, and with some authority, "was left by one of the undead. That's an undead footprint if ever I saw one."

"S-so what about the things we left behind us when we ran for it? I mean, the undead couldn't eat a herring—could they? They wouldn't want a wooden leg. All they'd want's a dead leg."

"Probably just hurled them away somewhere in anger and frustration. Like up onto the roof of the church. I bet they're up there on the top of the bell tower."

Tim looked toward the bell tower. All the unease of darkness had returned to him.

"Of course, the undead don't come out during the day, do they, Thruppence?" he said.

"Who told you that?" she said.

"You mean, they do? How come you know so much about them?"

"It was all in one of those books at the Ministry of Ghosts. It said in there that you can run into the undead at any time. Morning, noon, or night. In the park. On your way to school . . ."

"We're on our way to school," Tim said.

Thruppence looked at her watch.

"Yes, we ought to be going," she said, "or we'll be late."

"Tell you what," Tim said, looking down at the enormous footprint. "Let's run."

"Yeah," Thruppence said, following his gaze. "Not a bad idea."

So, just as they had the previous night, they turned and fled from the graveyard as fast as they could go.

17
MAN IN BLACK

A man in dark clothes, the somberness and severity of which were only broken by the whiteness of his collar, marched down Bric-a-Brac Street with the air of one on a mission.

Approaching the door of the Ministry of Ghosts, he broke his stride, stopped, hesitated, almost raised his arm to ring the bell or to pound the knocker, but felt uncertain.

What made him pause were the instructions by the door, which still read, as they always had: VISITORS BY APPOINTMENT ONLY. DELIVERIES—PLEASE RING BELL.

The man did not have an appointment nor was he delivering anything. So what to do? How did one make an appointment without knocking? No telephone number was advertised. And if appointments could not be made then how did anyone ever get to speak to those inside?

But, on the other hand, perhaps he *was* delivering something after all. He was the bearer of tidings, was he not? He came with news. He carried in a large duffle bag in his hand two curious objects, which might be of vast interest to those inside. So yes, maybe he was in the delivery business. The bell then. That would be the thing.

So he rang it. He heard it burble away in the depths of the building, and he waited for someone to respond to its summons.

As he waited, the man looked up and down the street. In appearance, he was prepossessing. He was large and had a thick neck, and he had the build of a bouncer, a wrestler, or a heavyweight boxer. His features matched his dimensions for his jaw hung like a lantern, his nose appeared to have had past encounters with various fists, his teeth were missing here and there, and there was a scar above his eye. He also had one ear like a cauliflower while the other ear was more like a beetroot.

All things considered, the man was not one you would have cared to encounter when alone on a dark night.

And yet appearances may be deceiving.

The man reached up and rang the bell again. His first summons had not been answered. Maybe it had not been heard.

As he waited, he studied the gleaming brass plate on the wall.

It was an odd thing, but the man, though something of a newcomer to the area, having been there only a matter of weeks, had already walked down Bric-a-Brac Street on several occasions. He had walked back up it, too. Yet he had never realized that such a place as the Ministry of Ghosts was right there in his own neighborhood.

He had noticed the cobwebbed windows and the dusty half-shutters and he had always assumed the building was empty and derelict, awaiting redevelopment or to be the subject of some disputed will.

It was only a couple of days ago that the man had noticed the shiny brass plate. The sight of it had stopped him, and he had stood wonderingly, raising a thick, stubby finger to trace the letters engraved there.

"The Ministry of Ghosts . . ." He had said the words out loud. "Well, imagine that."

For the large man in the dark suit had a personal and vested interest in that line of work. But he had reason to call beyond mere curiosity. For in the bag he held was possible evidence of supernatural visitation, and he needed to consult with the experts.

Thus, losing hope in the bell, he turned his hand to the knocker, and such was the strength within his large boned knuckles that his summons could no longer be denied.

The door swung open. Its creak had all but gone. Oiled by the entries and exits of ever more frequent visitors, it had become smooth and silent.

"Good morning. Can I help you?"

Mrs. Scant found herself looking up at a man who towered above her like some piece of recently erected scaffolding, which had not been there earlier when she had arrived for work. She noticed the contrast between his rough build and features and the smoothness of his apparel—his neat black suit, his bright white collar. And then there was the large bag in his hand.

"Good morning," the man said. "The Reverend Reggie Mangle, vicar of St. Bindle's—just down the way. The local church."

"Oh, charmed, I'm sure," Mrs. Scant said, though she wasn't actually sure of that at all. For Reverend Mangle may have had the clothes of a cleric, but he had the look of an armed and dangerous bank robber.

The reverend seemed immediately aware of this. Perhaps it was a prejudice he had encountered before. He spoke, anxious to put Mrs. Scant at her ease.

"Please, good lady," he said, "do not be put off by this rough and ready exterior. Inside, I assure you, is a man of faith. True, I once followed the road of ease and dalliance and took what was not mine wherever I fancied. But I long since saw the light—"

"Oh, the light. Saw that, did you?" Mrs. Scant said. "It's good to see the light."

"Better the light than to stumble along in the darkness," Reverend Mangle said.

"Absolutely," Mrs. Scant said. "Or you could whack your shins on the furniture."

"I'm afraid I do not have an appointment," Reverend Mangle said, "but I would like, if possible, to make one. Or, better still, to consult with your best man, or woman of course, right away—should they have a few minutes to spare."

"Oh, well, I don't know—" Mrs. Scant began.

But then Reverend Mangle leaned his bulk forward, raised a large, hairy hand to the side of his mouth, exposed one or two gold fillings, and said, in closest confidence so that no one else might hear, "I believe I may have some evidence of ghostly activity," he said.

Mrs. Scant's eyebrows arched high in astonishment, like caterpillars doing aerobics.

"Really?" she said. "You've . . . seen a ghost?"

"No," Reverend Mangle said. "But I may have heard them. And I have possible evidence in this bag here of their presence and their mysterious doings."

"Oh, mysterious doings," Mrs. Scant said. "Well, that's what we're here to investigate. I think you'd better come in for a moment, and I'll see if Mr. Copperstone is free."

"Thank you, ma'am," the good man said, and he followed her inside, into the cool shade of the Ministry, and Mrs. Scant left him to wait in a small foyer while she went to see if Mr. Copperstone was awake enough to welcome visitors.

"Mr. Copperstone . . ."

But he was fully conscious and not nodding off at all.

"Mrs. Scant?"

"Gentleman, sir, at the door just now. A tall, reverend gentleman, of the cloth—"

"The cloth, Mrs. Scant?"

"Vicar of St. Bindle's, he says. The local parish church."

"I know it well, Mrs. Scant, I was b—" But then Mr. Copperstone stopped in mid-sentence for some reason. "But, please continue, Mrs. Scant."

"He says he might have some evidence with him of . . . ghostly activity, sir."

"Ghostly activity, Mrs. Scant? Really? Well, that's splendid. You must show him up immediately. And ask

Miss Rolly and Mr. Gibbings to come up, too. This could be exciting news, Mrs. Scant. Our jobs ... the Ministry ..."

"We could be saved, sir?"

"We could certainly. Please—show him up at once."

Mrs. Scant did as requested, and she, too, was invited to stay for the meeting. So she took her place in Mr. Copperstone's office, along with Miss Rolly, Mr. Gibbings, and Reverend Reggie Mangle—his large, imposing self and his large, imposing duffle bag.

"Please," Mr. Copperstone said, once the introductions and formalities were complete, "tell us what is on your mind."

"Very well," the reverend said. "It's like this. For the past ten years, since I got out of pris—that is, since I saw the light, I have worked and studied to become a minister and was given the parish of St. Bindle's a little while ago."

"Nice," Mr. Copperstone said, trying to look interested, though he wasn't. He just wanted the vicar to get to the ghost part.

"The afterlife and the world beyond have always been an interest of mine, and I have long suspected that ghostly activity has been going on in St. Bindle's parish, but I was never able to track it down."

"Really?" Mr. Copperstone said. "Ghostly activity? Here? You feel that?"

"It's a kind of sixth sense I've got," Reverend Reggie said. "I've always had it. That's why I was so good in the boxing ring. I could tell where the punches were coming from before they arrived . . ." He ruefully touched his slightly flattened nose and his hand moved to his cauli-flower ear. "Except for a couple of times," he said.

"Please continue," Mr. Copperstone said.

"Anyway, I've had the feeling for a long time that there are ghosts in St. Bindle's parish, and not just one, but a few of them."

"Are they up to no good, do you think?" Mr. Gibbings asked.

"I couldn't really say," the reverend answered. "They might be bad ghosts; they might be good. In fact, I don't think they do much at all. But they're there, hanging around, and who knows what they've got in mind?"

"So . . . something happened recently?" Mr. Copperstone said.

"Yes, it did," Reverend Mangle said.

"Bumps in the night?" Miss Rolly asked.

"Sort of."

"Apparitions?" Mrs. Scant said.

"Kind of."

"This all sounds very promising. Please continue," Mr. Copperstone said.

"Well, last night, I was asleep in the vicarage, which is right next to the church. Mrs. Mangle—"

"Oh, there's a Mrs. Mangle, is there?" Mr. Copperstone said, with a note of surprise.

"There is," the reverend said. "And a splendid woman she is, too."

"No doubt."

"And there is also a small Mangle, aged two years, one month."

"Oh."

"And another Mangle on the way."

"A Mangle on the way. Well, that is good news," Mr. Copperstone said. "Isn't it, Mrs. Scant? One can never have too many Mangles."

She tried to look as if she thought it was good news, but in truth, she didn't care either way.

"Now, although our view of the church graveyard is blocked by the church itself, we can still hear things going on there, even if we can't see them."

"Yes?"

"Anyway, last night, I was wakened shortly after midnight by the sound of eerie voices—"

"Eerie voices?"

"Almost like the voices of ghostly children—"

"Ghostly children?"

"And they seemed to be chanting this weird and primitive chant—"

"Really?" Mr. Copperstone said. "So not just weird, but primitive, too?"

"Anyway, I woke up Mrs. Mangle with a soft poke of the elbow—"

"I'm glad it was just a soft one," Mr. Copperstone said.

"And I said, 'Do you hear that?'"

"And did she?" Mr. Copperstone asked.

"She did. So I got up, and I went to the window, and though I could see nothing, because of the church being between us and the graveyard, I could make out this faint glow of light—like a candle burning."

"A candle!"

"And I thought to myself: bell, book, and candle, I thought. There's something going on here. So I got my robe and I said to Mrs. Mangle, 'I'm going to investigate, my dear. You wait here, where you'll be safe.'"

"'Reggie,' she said, 'is this wise?' I said, 'A vicar has to do what a vicar has to do.' And then I kissed her goodbye, in case I should never return, and I went down and put on my rain boots, and I picked up my Bible—the very heavy one that's good for trouble—and out I went into the night."

"Good heavens," Mrs. Scant said. "What a brave man."

"I was only doing my duty," Reggie Mangle said modestly.

"But all the same," Mrs. Scant said. "Fearless, I call it. Fearless."

"So out I went into the night, like I said. The chanting noise had stopped, but the glow of light was still there, leaking around the stones of the church walls in the dark. I moved forward, stepping careful and trying to keep quiet. But then, just as I was coming up behind the yew tree, I stepped on a stick, and it cracked like a gunshot, and I stumbled and tripped a bit. By the time I was steady again, the next thing I heard were ghostly voices and rustling and commotions, and by the time I was out from behind the bush, the ghosts or apparitions, or whatever they were, had fled."

"Oh," Mr. Copperstone said, disappointed.

"But they left some things behind. Let me show you. See what you make of this. May I?"

And Reverend Mangle hoisted up the duffle bag with one hand and set it upon Mr. Copperstone's desk.

As the others watched closely, he pulled back the zipper, and then he extracted from the bag two strange objects.

The first was a wooden leg.

And the second was a herring.

"I put the herring in that plastic sandwich bag myself," the reverend explained. "When I found it, it was just lying on the ground. So, what do you make of that? I mean, if this is the Ministry of Ghosts then you must be the ghost experts. So, what's a wooden leg and a herring doing in the graveyard after midnight? Is that spooky or what?"

There was a silence. Mr. Copperstone's staff looked at him, wondering what he might say. None of them actually knew that their Weekend Boy and their Weekend Girl had been out in the graveyard ghost hunting the night before, but it didn't take much to put two and two together and to surmise that they had and that Reverend Mangle had disturbed them and they had fled, leaving some of their equipment behind.

"Well . . ." Mr. Copperstone didn't quite know how to go on after that. Then he had a thought. "What might be your theory, Reverend?" he said.

"Levitation," Reverend Mangle said. "You know how ghosts are supposed to be able to move things around by the mere power of the mind—"

"I have heard—"

"Opening doors and banging drawers and emptying closets and flinging the contents around and scaring cats and—"

"Yes, yes, we are familiar with the basics, Reverend."

"Yes, of course you are. Anyway, my theory is that there are ghosts in the graveyard of people buried there. I reckon that one of them had a craving for herring."

"A craving for herring? Well, it's a possibility."

"And the other lost a leg in some old battle, say the Battle of Waterloo, maybe, back in eighteen fifteen."

"That is a long time ago," Mr. Gibbings said.

"There are gravestones in the cemetery even older than that," Reverend Mangle informed him. "So, I reckon that he has laid in his grave for a very long time, but he has not rested easy, because when they buried him, they did not include his wooden leg along with the rest. And so he can never find peace or move on to the next life until he gets his wooden leg back—or a substitute very much like it."

"It's a plausible theory," Mr. Copperstone conceded. "But—"

"And as for the herring," Reverend Mangle said, "my theory is that a ghost in the graveyard had levitated that herring all the way from Good Coddley's Fish Shop— if you know it. It's the local fishmonger's. I believe that somewhere in the graveyard is buried a person whose last wish was to eat a herring before they died."

"Eat a herring?" Mr. Copperstone said. "It is a some-what unusual final request—"

"And maybe they'd even asked for a herring, and the herring was on the way, and maybe even the very knife and fork was in their hands, and the herring was right there on the plate, and they were just about to take a mouthful, when—bang!"

"Bang?"

"They died. And they never did get their herring at the end. And so now, they can't move on to the next life either, because they haven't had their herring."

"Not had their herring," Mr. Copperstone echoed. And he looked around the room at his staff, who were maintaining admirably blank expressions and straight faces.

"And that ghost will not be at peace until a herring is there with him, lying by his side in his final resting place," Reverend Mangle said. "And the same applies to the wooden leg. But as I don't know what grave the herring and the wooden leg belong to, there's nothing I can do. Otherwise, I'd do my best to help them and get a shovel. But I can't go burying a herring in the wrong grave, can I? That would upset the person in there, if it was the wrong place. And then they'd start haunting the cemetery, too, because they'd had a herring buried with them and they didn't want it there. So I've come here for advice. What do you think I should do now? Should I hang onto the herring, or should I bury it, or should I take it back to the vicarage and give it to the cat? I know it's been on the ground, but a cat wouldn't worry about that. Cats'll eat anything. Off the ground or not. So, what do you think?"

Mr. Copperstone made a steeple of his fingers and peered through them at Reverend Mangle.

"Reverend," he began, "first, I would like to applaud your actions in bringing these matters to our attention. You have come to the right people."

"Yeah, though funnily enough I didn't know you were even here until recently, when someone must have polished up your brass plate. I thought the place was empty."

"Quite. But my thoughts are that you should leave these articles with us here, and we will look into them . . ."

"Oh, would you?" Reverend Mangle said, with both relief and gratitude. "It's such a busy parish, I've got so much to do, and to take on one more thing—"

"Not at all. You leave your leg and your herring with us, Reverend, and we shall get to the bottom of this. Yes, we shall get to the bottom of your leg and we shall get to the bottom of your herring as soon as we can. And if we are unable to get to the bottom of them, we will figure out the reason why."

"Then I shall do as you say," Reverend Mangle said, rising to his rather enormous feet, the ones that had so startled Thruppence Coddley and Tim Legge in St. Bindle's Church cemetery the previous night. "If you'll excuse me, I must do my rounds and visit my parishioners. I must go and bring comfort to the elderly around at the Dun Working Rest Home for Seniors, and then when I've finished that, I need to be getting to the hospital to cheer up the patients in intensive care. And then I have to call in at the school one day this week and chat with the children. I've not been there yet. Too busy."

"Don't let us keep you from your good work," Mr. Copperstone said, rising to usher Reverend Mangle to the door. "Mrs. Scant will see you downstairs, I'm sure. Thank you for having come to us to report these matters.

If only the rest of the public were as diligent and as fearless and as observant as you."

"Not at all," Reverend Mangle said modestly. And he bade goodbye to Miss Rolly and Mr. Gibbings, and then Mrs. Scant saw him down the stairs to the front door. He took his now empty duffle bag with him.

"I do apologize for not offering you any tea," Mrs. Scant said. "It totally slipped my mind."

"Not a problem," the reverend said. "I'm awash with tea most of the day. Endless offers of tea and cakes, everywhere I go."

He patted his stomach, as if to say one must try to lay off the cake and to keep the weight down. And then he was off, and the door was shut behind him.

What a nice man, Mrs. Scant thought. *Rather intimidating on a first encounter, but charming when you get to know him. Pity about his cauliflower ear, but then vegetables are supposed to be good for you.*

18
FURTHER SEARCHING

The loss of one old wooden leg from the storage cellar of The Legge Works was of no great importance to Tim Legge's father. He hadn't even noticed its absence and probably never would.

The cellar was stacked with remnants from a bygone era, objects that the family business had once produced but for which there was no longer any demand.

Wooden legs—who wanted them? Wooden yokes for milkmaids, which were used to suspend two wooden pails, for the carrying of full cream milk—who needed them? Wooden frames for hitching up four fine horses together so that they could pull some gentleman's carriage along the street—well, you could start your car up now, couldn't you, or hop on your skateboard, or get on your bike.

At Good Coddley's, it was similarly unlikely that Thruppence Coddley's father, George, was going to notice that he was short of a herring.

He had so many herrings there, in the fridge, in the cool room, in vacuum-sealed bags, hanging up in the smokehouse, that he would no more feel the loss of one herring than a billionaire would feel the loss of a penny.

So neither Tim nor Thruppence was really worried that having abandoned these things in St. Bindle's grave-yard the night before was going to get them into any trouble. But what they had seen there, what they had heard, and the sight and sound of the appalling, flat-footed, asthmatic monster (otherwise known as Reverend Reggie Mangle) stayed with them throughout the day.

"We're going to have to be more careful next time," Thruppence said to Tim, when they spoke briefly at recess.

"What do you mean, next time?" he said.

"Well, we can't give up just because we've had a minor setback, can we? Or just because we ran into the undead? We've still got a job to do and ghosts to find and people depending on us to do it."

"Yeah, maybe, but—"

"So let's go back to the Ministry this afternoon, and we can fill them in on what's happened, and then get another look at Grimes and Natterly's *Manual of Ghost Hunting*."

"Yes, but—"

"Or are you getting cold feet, Tim? Is that it? Would you rather that I went and caught a ghost on my own?"

Tim did his best to look offended and show some dignity.

"Of course I'm not saying that. I'm seeing this through right to the end. When Tim Legge says he'll do something . . ."

"Yes?"

"Then he does it, usually, eventually, though it can sometimes take a while."

"I'll see you by the front door of the Ministry after the final bell rings this afternoon."

"Yes, but Thruppence, what about last night? That thing that was coming for us, that big, horrible zombie thing that was making all the wheezing noises and that we heard shuffling through the cemetery like it was one of the living dead!"

"It was just one of the living dead, that's all! I've been telling you that all day."

"Yes, and what if it comes back for us? What if it saw our faces? What if it knows where we live?"

But just then, a large figure with huge hands and great (flat) feet, all dressed in somber black, came lumbering through the gates of Eustace Scool School.

Tim saw him first.

"Thruppence! Thruppence! Look! It's come for us! The undead—he's back!"

Thruppence's eyes followed Tim's and gazed to where his extended arm and trembling hand pointed. For a second she, too, experienced a wave of fright—well, maybe more than that; it was terror. She, too, for a moment believed that the end had actually come. But then, as the huge, horrible monster turned around to politely ask a student where the teacher might be found, she saw the flash of white collar around the apparition's throat. A flash of white, clerical collar.

"Tim—it's the new vicar."

"What?"

"It must be. They said at the assembly there was a new one and he'd be coming here to say hello. That must be him."

"So that was the vicar we saw in the graveyard last night?"

"He must have heard us. We must have woken him up, and he came out to investigate. It's not the undead after all; it's the vicar. My mistake, but anyone can make one."

"Well, I don't think vicars should be allowed to look like that," Tim said. "I don't think it's right that vicars should go around looking like pro wrestlers and great big undead zombies that someone's just dug up from a hole in the ground. If a vicar's going to be a vicar, he should look like one. He should have a bald head with a bit of hair around the outsides and be a bit tubby and have fat fingers and a big smile, and he should go around saying, 'Bless you.' He shouldn't be seven feet tall and have feet like tennis rackets."

Reverend Mangle spotted the teacher at the far end of the yard and hurried over to greet her. On his way he passed Tim and Thruppence, but he gave no sign of recognition. He just said good morning to them, and then smiled and gave them a view of his gold teeth and the gaps among them, where action in the boxing ring had dislodged a couple of incisors.

"He seems nice enough to me," Thruppence said.

"For one of the undead," Tim added.

And then the bell rang, and recess was over.

• • •

Thruppence reached up, put her key into the lock, and turned it. She walked into the cool shadows of the vestibule with Tim Legge following behind her.

"Hello! Anyone in? We're here?"

"We're up here having a meeting! Please, come on up!" old Mr. Copperstone's voice called.

Up they went to the office where they found Mr. Copperstone behind his desk, facing Mrs. Scant, Miss Rolly, and Mr. Gibbings.

On Mr. Copperstone's desk was a wooden leg, and next to it, in a plastic bag and starting to smell slightly, was a herring.

"Ah!" Thruppence said. "I see you've got our stuff."

"Reverend Mangle found them and brought them over," Mr. Copperstone said. "He seemed to think that it might have something to do with ghostly activities in his cemetery."

"Well, it did, sort of," Thruppence said.

"Can I have my leg back?" Tim asked.

"We were trying to trap a ghost last night," Thruppence explained, "all according to the manual, but Reverend Mangle interrupted us—not that we knew it was him."

"No. We thought he was a big bogey," Tim said. "Though when I say bogey, I don't mean the kind of bogey that you'd find up your no—"

"I don't think you need to elaborate, Tim," Thruppence said. "I think we know what you mean."

"Just saying," Tim said.

Mr. Copperstone steepled his hands in his thoughtful way.

"So, you had no luck in the cemetery?" he said. "Ghost-wise?"

"No," Thruppence said. "But that doesn't mean we're giving up. We're going to take another look at the ghost-hunting manual, if that's all right with you, and then we're going to soldier on."

At this Miss Rolly bubbled over with excitement and enthusiasm and approval.

"Oh, what a fine young lady this girl is," she exclaimed. "What pluck, what courage, what character, what determination! This is the sort of girl the suffragette movement needs. A few more like her and all the barriers of discrimination will just crumble away!"

There was a bit of an embarrassed silence in the room after that. Mr. Copperstone didn't say as much, but he plainly did not approve of these outbursts. And yet he did not wish to reprimand Miss Rolly, especially not in front of others. For he regarded her as a valuable member of the team and would never wish to demean or to lose her. Also, he was a little frightened of her.

"Yes, well, anyway . . ." Mr. Copperstone said. "If, um . . . you'd like to . . . to take your leg away, Tim."

"Of course. Thanks. Sorry for any inconvenience."

"Not at all. And as for the herring. . ."

"It's probably not good for much by now," Thruppence said. "I'll take it away and throw it in the garbage."

"Thank you."

"We'll go down to the library now and have another look at Grimes and Natterly's *Manual of Ghost Hunting*. See if there's anything else we can try."

"Please avail yourselves of anything there," Mr. Copperstone said. "Might I also recommend Snodge and

Bickerstuff's *Encyclopedia of Spooks*. You'll find it on the shelves there. It also has a few pages on ghost hunting and is especially good for information on haunted houses and how to get a mortgage on one."

"We'll take a look at everything, thanks. Coming, Tim?"

"Just getting my leg."

So Tim took his leg, and Thruppence retrieved her herring, and down to the library they went.

They spent an hour or more poring through the books there, jotting down recommended methods for the finding, the luring, and the capturing of ghosts.

"Okay," Thruppence said, putting down her pen. "I think we've gotten enough here to help us continue our search. I ought to go home now, or my parents be wondering where I am."

She and Tim called their goodbyes to the people upstairs and went out into the street. Thruppence dropped the old herring into a trash can. Then they turned a corner, and who should they see coming toward them but Reverend Mangle.

"Tim! The leg!"

Tim quickly hid it behind his back. Reverend Mangle passed them without so much as a nod. He appeared to be distracted, and his mind, no doubt, was preoccupied with the affairs of his parish. For he had more to worry about than herrings and wooden legs. There was the Men's Club, the Women's League, the Sunday School, the Coffee Morning, the Harvest Festival; there were weddings, there were funerals, there were baptisms—it went on and on. Looking back to his past life, he sometimes felt that things had been a lot easier when he was robbing banks, with a sawn-off shotgun in one hand and a large pickax handle in the other.

But, fortunately, he had seen the light.

• • •

Over the new few weeks, Thruppence Coddley and Tim Legge, both together and separately, tried many plans to find and trap a ghost.

They held a séance; they made an Ouija board; they tried again with spells and incantations; they went to dark and frightening places; but all to no avail.

They even tried a haunted house. This was an old and empty building in Brewery Row, the doors and windows of which were all boarded up and had been for years. But there was a loose panel at the back, which they pried away to allow them entry.

It was said that both a murder and a suicide had taken place here at number seventeen many years ago. It was said that a poor woman, ground down by years of hunger and poverty and unable to look after her children, had first killed her landlady downstairs, who was threatening her with eviction, and had then killed herself—while her children were gone. She had left a misspelled note saying: "*Theyl be beter off wivout me. Beter a live in the wurkhuse than a live like thiss.*"

But, in its anguish, the poor woman's ghost was said to have returned, and it stalked the house, searching in every room and in every nook and cranny and cupboard and in every inch of the cellar and loft for those lost and abandoned children.

"Where are you, my dears?" the ghost supposedly said. "I'm so sorry I left you. So sorry I did. Come to me now, my dears. Come to your mother's arms."

Doors were banged open and shut, and windows rattled, and old furniture moved as the ghost went eternally through the house, searching, always searching, for those lost, abandoned children.

But now, when Thruppence and Tim crept into the house, with flashlights in their hands and with their courage screwed up tight, with their ghost-hunting gear and with their ghost trap—the thick glass jar with the stopper, inside of which, for bait, they had placed a baby's rattle, which had come from Thruppence's drawer of her own memorabilia—there was nothing but silence. An eerie, awful, frightening silence. But silence all the same.

The ghost did not come to them. She did not cry out for her children. She did not slam the doors or make the windows tremble. She just kept her grief and pain to herself, and made no sound.

Maybe she was waiting for them to leave; maybe she saw in them two young and decent people, who reminded her so painfully much of her own lost children, and so she did not care to frighten or to harm them in any way.

Or maybe she was not there. And never had been. And it was all just a story, the whole thing: the murder, the suicide, the children, the ghost—all fantasy, all gossip and rumor, the product of idle tongues and overactive imaginations.

Yes. Maybe the truth of it is that there are no ghosts—anywhere. Nowhere in the world at all. All that's there is the human desire to be startled and amazed and to believe that there are farther and greater things that exist than just in dull, solid form. A world without ghosts. A world without possibility. A world without magic and mystery—what good is that?

But all the same, it did not look good. Tim and Thruppence did their best, but after each venture they went home empty-handed with nothing in the jar but the bait.

And so time moved on, and the deadline was approaching, and soon Mr. Beeston would return to the Ministry and he would demand evidence and sight of a real-live ghost. And if one could not be produced then that was the end. It was the end of the Ministry and the end of Mr. Copperstone, who would be bundled away to tedious retirement and empty days of monotony and boredom. And Miss Rolly and Mrs. Scant and Mr. Gibbings would be posted to the Ministry of Sewage to end their careers amid the splashes and the odors and the unpleasant glugs that would come from the processing plant next door.

Nevertheless, Mr. Copperstone ensured that the two children were paid promptly, as agreed. Their money was always there waiting for them when they let themselves in on Friday afternoons. Two envelopes. One marked *Thruppence*, one marked *Tim*, in thin, scrawly handwriting—Mr. Copperstone's, one presumed.

And Tim and Thruppence each pocketed their wages. But not with the delight that you might assume. Because they had not succeeded in their work or in their quest.

And they did so want to succeed. They discovered—to their surprise—that they wanted to find a ghost and to save the Ministry and old Mr. Copperstone and his staff far more than anything else.

"I don't know what it is, Thruppence," Tim said, "because I thought I'd be very happy to be making all this money, but somehow . . . it's not so great now. I can't find any fun in it. It just feels—not very good somehow."

"I know what you mean, Tim," Thruppence said. "I just take mine home and hide it in the drawer. I don't want to spend it or anything."

"Me neither," Tim said. "I let it stack up, but I just don't care about it somehow. All I want to do is do the right thing—to find a ghost for them."

"Me, too," Thruppence said. "I might enjoy the money once I've done that. But until then . . ."

"How long have we got left now?" Tim asked.

"Just over three weeks," Thruppence said.

"So that's more than two months we've been looking. And still no luck."

"But we can't have tried everything," Thruppence said. "We can't have exhausted all the possibilities. There must have been something we've missed. There must have. I bet there is, Tim. I bet there is something and it's staring us right in the face."

"Like a can't see the wood for the trees kind of thing," Tim said.

"Exactly. Come on. Let's go through all the books again. There has to be something we've missed, Tim. There just has to be."

And, in saying that, Thruppence Coddley was absolutely correct. There was something that she and Tim Legge had missed. There was something staring both of them right in the face. Yet, both of them were blind to it and were likely to remain that way forever.

Unless . . .

Oh yes, of course.

Unless . . .

But meanwhile, there was one other solution. Because, even if you cannot find a ghost, even if you cannot produce one to show to your boss and superiors for their staff appraisals, there is something else you can do. You can *pretend* that you have found one.

You can fool them, if you have to, with a hoax.

19
A JAR OF GHOST

It's not from lack of trying on our part, Mr. Copperstone," Thruppence said.

"I didn't think that for a moment, my dear," Mr. Copperstone told her. "I know that you have done more than your best."

Thruppence, Tim, and Mr. Copperstone were huddled together for a meeting in his office. It was late on a Wednesday afternoon.

"We've looked everywhere. Left no stone unturned," Thruppence went on.

"And that's in the ghost-hunting book, too—*Spells for the Upturning of Stones: Large Ones*," Tim said.

"Once or twice we felt we were getting so close—"

"You could feel it," Tim said. "The hairs standing up on the back of your neck."

"But when it came to it—"

"Nothing there."

"A feeling, certainly—"

"But you can't trap feelings in a glass jar," Tim pointed out. "So, we're back here again and empty-handed, too, again, I'm afraid."

"But it's not for lack of trying," Thruppence repeated.

"We can assure you of that. We were out last night looking for ghosts down at the soccer field—"

"For the ghosts of soccer players past," Tim explained. "Who died before they were able to score that winning goal and who walk the field in anguish, unable to be at rest until they've put things right, wanting some extra time and another shot at the net. But the ghosts must have been playing an away game last night, as none of them were there."

Mr. Copperstone was silent a while, his steepled fingers resting against each other, their immobility reflecting his steadiness of thought.

"You know," he said, "I am starting to wonder if perhaps that awful Mr. Beeston was possibly right. What if there really are no ghosts?"

"No!" Thruppence said.

"No!" Tim agreed.

"No, that's impossible. We know they're there. We've felt them, even maybe glimpsed them . . ." Thruppence trailed off.

"But what . . . what if . . . well . . . we allow ourselves to imagine such things? What if the Ministry of Ghosts has truly been a place without purpose and all our labors have been in vain since the Ministry was founded, back in nineteen seventy-two—I mean, seventeen ninety-two. I was never great at math."

"No, that can't be right, Mr. Copperstone," Thruppence said. "The ghosts are there. You can feel it in your very, well, your very . . ."

"Bones?" Tim suggested.

"Yes, and in your heart, too," Thruppence said. "We just need a little more time, that's all."

"It's of the essence, time is," Tim said. (It was an expression he had heard on several occasions and he liked the sound of it.)

"You may be correct," Mr. Copperstone said. "But time is what we do not have. The beast Beeston will be back next week. If we do not have a ghost to show him, well . . . he will be implacable."

"Will he?" Tim said. "That's not so good. By the way, what does implacable mean?"

"It means he will stubbornly continue with his plans to shut down the Ministry and to send us on our way— either to retirement or to the administration of sewage."

"Oh. I see."

The three of them were silent now, until Thruppence, after a glance at Tim and a nod of assent back from him, broached their alternative plan. "Mr. Copperstone . . ."

"Hmm?" he said, distracted and lost in thought.

"There is a way of buying some time."

"What might that be, my dear?"

"Well—you know that story, *The Emperor's New Clothes*?"

"Hans Christian Andersen! I remember it well. My mother used to tell it to me back when I was in knickerbockers."

"What are—?"

"Not now, please, Tim," Thruppence hissed.

"I mean, I know what knickers are," Tim whispered back. "But I'm a bit stuck on the bockers."

"Later, Tim."

"Oh, all right."

"But what," Mr. Copperstone said, "do the emperor's new clothes have to do with us?"

"Easy, Mr. Copperstone. In the story, the emperor had no clothes on. The swindlers had sold the emperor a suit of nothing. But they told him that only wise and intelligent people could see it. So everyone pretended they could see the suit, because they didn't want to seem stupid."

"And?"

"Well, what if we hand Mr. Beeston a glass jar with a stopper on it, and we say—or rather *you* say, as obviously we won't be here—that there it is. There's your ghost!"

A wide smile spread across Mr. Copperstone's face.

"Oh, what an idea," he said. "What a delicious—and possibly rather wicked, not of course that you are wicked, my dear, quite the contrary—"

"I always smell of strawberries, actually," Thruppence said. "Fresh ones."

"Yes. But do you think Mr. Beeston would be fooled?"

"For a while, maybe. And while he's working out what's going on, it gives us more time to find a real ghost."

"I see. Yes. So you think that when Beeston gets here, I should show him a glass jar with a stopper in it and say, 'There it is, Mr. Beeston. There's your ghost!'"

"Exactly."

"Well, what an idea. Now why can't I think of clever things like this?" Mr. Copperstone said.

"'Cause you're too old," Tim informed him.

"Tim!" Thruppence shouted.

"Nothing personal. Just saying."

"No, he's probably right, Thruppence. And I do feel old some days. I feel about a hundred and fifty some mornings. But never mind. All right, I'm of a mind to give your idea a try. But I think we should have a little something in the jar. Maybe a little smoke or something. Or some dust. Just to give things a touch of authenticity. Would you be able to arrange that?"

"You leave it to us, Mr. Copperstone. We'll fix up a jar so it looks convincing. And we'll bring it over so that you can have it in reserve, in case a ghost doesn't turn up between now and next Wednesday."

"Thank you. I feel a lot more optimistic now and easier in my mind. If nothing else, it will buy us some time. There could be a ghost just around the corner. Waiting there for us. A ghost with . . . what's that modern expression again?"

"A ghost with our names on it!" Tim and Thruppence said together.

"A ghost with our names on it. That's the one."

"All right," Thruppence said. "We'll get to work."

"And we'll keep looking for ghosts, too," Tim said.

"You can rely on us, Mr. Copperstone," Thruppence assured him. "We won't let you down. If anyone can keep you out of the sewage department, we can!"

"Thank you. That is most reassuring. And now . . ."

Mr. Copperstone plainly had a little work to finish before he went home. What that work might be, who could imagine? In truth Mr. Copperstone appeared to have nothing to do all day than to make steeples out of his fingers, to doze in his chair, and to have long chats with Mrs. Scant, which usually culminated in promises of tea that never arrived.

Before seeing themselves out, the two children went down to the library and the storage room to look around. Maybe there was something they had missed down there, some essential nugget of information. There were so many volumes on the subject of ghosts it would have been a lifetime's worth of reading to get through them all.

While Thruppence checked through the ghost-trapping equipment, Tim, in the adjacent room, thumbed through some books. First the ever reliable Grimes and Natterly's *Manual of Ghost Hunting*. Next, he turned the pages of Snodge and Bickerstuff's *Encyclopedia of Spooks*. Then, lodged under a pile of old newspapers and magazines, Tim spotted an edition he had not noticed before.

"Hey, Thruppence! Look at this."

She came over to see what he was excited about. But it was just another drab, leather-covered tome.

"Haven't we already seen that one?"

"No. Look. It's called: *101 Things You Never Knew About the Paranormal*."

"Is that going to help us, Tim? We really need—"

"Hold on. Just let me look up 'ghosts.'"

Tim consulted the index and turned to the appropriate page.

"Hey, now this is interesting," he said. "Look at this. I didn't know this, did you?"

Thruppence leaned over the book, and Tim smelled the faint perfume of fresh strawberries. It was remarkable how she managed that, seeing as her dad owned a fishmonger's shop and the family slept in an apartment right above it.

Little known facts about ghosts, the entry read:

1) Ghosts are, in most instances, not unfriendly. Ghosts do not wish to frighten people. Ghosts merely wish to be at peace and to find the means of achieving this.

2) Ghosts are affected by temperature. They become hyperactive in extreme heat and sluggish in cold. A ghost, if trapped, may be put in a freezer and can remain there indefinitely without harm. It will be as if the ghost has gone into hibernation. If taken from the freezer and allowed to warm up slowly, the ghost will become active again.

3) Ghosts, like vampires, do not cast reflections if viewed in mirrors. However, ghosts, unlike vampires, have no dislike of garlic, which is ineffective against them. Ghosts also cast no shadows, although they can often be of very solid appearance. It is a mistake to think that all ghosts are waif-like, transparent things. Some ghosts maybe very robust and may differ little from their appearance when living.

4) Ghosts are individuals. They differ in temperament just as the living do. Thus, while soft, sweet music may lure and entrap one kind of ghost, another will flee at the mere sound. And yet each ghost will have its weak spot, its Achilles' heel, just as do the living. For as in life, so in death and in the world beyond.

"Well, it's all very interesting," Thruppence said. "But I don't actually see that it helps."

"We haven't tried music yet for catching ghosts," Tim said.

"Okay, we'll give it a shot. But let's get this jar figured out first. How can we get smoke in a jar? That is, how can we get it to stay there?"

"We'll have to use something else."

"It has to be convincing. I mean, what does a ghost in a jar look like?"

"If it's invisible, it doesn't look like anything."

"We just need a touch of authenticity, that's all. Just a touch."

20

DEADLINE

It was three months to the day. The hard-faced and soberly dressed Mr. Franklin Beeston, OBE, MSc, and member of the Civil Service Squash and Tennis Club, hopped down from the bus at its termination point and headed with firm, deliberate steps towards Bric-a-Brac Street.

He noted with some small satisfaction the gleam upon the formerly shabby brass nameplate, and he saw that the handle of the knocker was brighter than before—yet not as if polished by a cloth so much as by use.

At least they've tidied the place up a bit, Mr. Beeston thought.

He took the door knocker and applied it to the wood with his usual firmness.

The door swung open, and Mrs. Scant invited him in. "Mr. Copperstone is expecting you, sir."

"So he should be."

"Shall I see you up, or . . . ?"

"No need. I know the way."

Up Mr. Beeston went, past the dull portraits and the mahogany tables, past old mirrors with their silver blemished and peeling away. As he went, the grandfather clock drummed him up the stairs, beating time like a bandsman at a military funeral.

"Mr. Beeston! Please! Take a seat."

"Copperstone!" Beeston said, not bothering with the formalities.

"So, how was your journey? It's a rather fine day today, is it not? The sunshine always seems—"

"Cut the time wasting, Copperstone. You know why I'm here. So let's see it. Let's see this ghost. Or maybe you haven't been able to find one—as I suspect will be the case. Looking for a ghost for over two hundred years, this Ministry. And have you found so much as a tiny little ghoul? It's a disgrace! A burden on the taxpayer. And it's high time that—"

"No, no, Mr. Beeston. I am pleased to say that we have a ghost for you, right here."

Mr. Copperstone pointed to an object on his desk, which looked rather like a small bird cage with a cover over it.

Mr. Beeston looked as if he was about to keel over. "You've found one?"

"Indeed we have."

"A ghost? A real one? A real ghost?"

"That is what I said."

"How? How did you catch it?"

"We outsourced the task to independent ghost hunters."

"You what?"

"Having had no success for ourselves, we thought it best to employ independent ghost hunters of a kind more likely to be attuned to the supernatural."

"And why didn't you think of this before?"

"Um, well . . ."

"Because you couldn't be bothered before. Because you needed a firework underneath you before you'd bother to do anything."

"We must agree to differ on that, Mr. Beeston, but here is your ghost right here."

Mr. Beeston looked at the covered object on the desk. "It's in there?"

"It is."

"Won't it escape if I take the cover off?"

"No, it is trapped inside a glass container. The cover is merely to keep it in the dark and to prevent it from growing agitated."

"Then let's have a look at it. You're sure it's safe?"

"It couldn't harm a wasp."

"What about a fly?"

"Not a fly either. It's securely imprisoned in the jar."

Mr. Beeston reached forward and slowly pulled the cover from the jar. The cover was lifted to reveal an object made of thick, blue-green glass, with a heavy glass stopper screwed in tight to its top.

But inside the jar . . . inside . . .

"Wait! Hold on! There's nothing in there!"

"My dear Mr. Beeston, the jar is full to the brim with a ghost!"

"Where?"

"Right there."

"I can't see anything."

"Can't you?"

"It's empty! That jar's flipping empty. There's nothing in there at all!"

"Well, plainly one needs a certain degree of insight and intelligence—"

"Are you calling me stupid?"

"Absolutely not. Certainly not, sir. Certainly not. I wouldn't dream—"

"Oh, hang on . . . I maybe see something now. What's that . . . that kind of oily stuff there, sort of smeared around the inside?"

"That is, no doubt, the residue that you can see, Mr. Beeston. That is residue of a ghost."

"Residue of a ghost?"

"I would imagine so. You trap a ghost in a confined space and it sort of . . . condenses out a little and leaves . . . a residue. In a confined space it is condensed and invisible, you see. Whereas with room to expand, you can see it whole."

"Oh. So this is a ghost, is it? In here? This here is a ghost?"

"Yes."

"Where did you find it?"

"Well, our ghost hunters found it for us. I think they got it outside the local school."

"School?"

"Apparently it was haunting the bicycle shed."

"The bicycle shed?"

"Looking for its long-lost bike."

"Looking for its long-lost bike? A ghost? Down at the bicycle shed? Looking for its bike?"

"They managed to trap it by sucking it up a bicycle pump, and then pumped it out into that jar then clamped the stopper tight before it could escape."

"Sucked it up a bicycle pump?"

"It's one of the tried and tested methods they use."

Mr. Beeston was lost for words. He sat, staring at the jar and shaking his head. Was this genuine? Was he being taken for a fool? Was someone making a joke at his expense?

He regained the power of speech.

"Now look, Copperstone. I'm not satisfied with this. You could be fooling me with an empty jar here for all I know. I'm going to have to send this off for analysis. And then we'll know the truth."

But Mr. Copperstone raised his hands in protest.

"My dear sir," he said, "you mustn't do that. If you send it away for analysis then someone will have to open the jar. And if you open the jar, the ghost will immediately . . . whoosh!"

"Whoosh?"

"Yes, whoosh! The ghost will be off like greased lightning! Never to be seen again. Or, possibly, off to the nearest bicycle shed to resume searching for its bike."

Mr. Beeston glared at Mr. Copperstone with the beadiest of eyes.

"Okay," he said. "So, you're telling me that there is a ghost in this jar. But if I try to check if there is a ghost in this jar then the ghost will escape from the jar, and I will no longer be able to check it?"

"It is a bit of a problem," Mr. Copperstone said. "And I do see the dilemma. But nobody said ghosts were easy."

"All right," Mr. Beeston said. "You might think you're pretty clever here, Copperstone. But here's what I'm going to do. I'm going to send this jar to the Medical Research Laboratories."

"Oh yes?" Mr. Copperstone said casually, but feeling uneasy.

"You know what they have there? They have an isolation room. You know what that room is made of?"

"Not glass, by any chance?"

"Glass! Glass walls, floor, ceiling, and a secure glass door. And I am going to send this jar there and have it opened. And when the ghost comes out, it won't be going anywhere, as it will be trapped in the glass room. And as it will have expanded, they will be able to see it. And if they don't see it . . ."

"If they don't see it?"

"I will then know for certain, Mr. Copperstone, that you have been trying to pull a fast one. And if my suspicions are confirmed, and such proves to be the case, then I shall be back. And when I return, I shall come down upon this useless Ministry like a ton of bricks!"

"Bricks? Really? A ton of them? That's a lot."

"You'd better believe it. And heads will roll, Mr. Copperstone. Heads will most certainly roll. And may I inform you that your head will be among the first to start the rolling."

Mr. Copperstone gulped, but he endeavored to keep an outer appearance of calm.

"Well, all I can tell you, sir," he said, "is that my ghost hunters assure me there is a ghost in that jar. Beyond that, I know no more than you do."

"Then we shall see," Mr. Beeston said. "We shall see." He re-covered the jar with the cloth bag.

"You'll be careful not to drop—"

"Don't worry. And you may have got yourself a bit of a reprieve here, Copperstone, but not for long. I'll have this uncorked within the week. One week's grace. That's all you've got. I'll be back. Have no fear of that. I'll be back."

But Beeston's return was just what Mr. Copperstone *did* fear.

As Mr. Beeston turned to go on his way, Mrs. Scant appeared at the office door and politely inquired, "Will you and your visitor be requiring a cup of tea, Mr. Copperstone?"

"Tea!" Beeston snarled, grasping the covered jar with the alleged ghost in it and heading for the stairs. "I haven't got time for tea. I can't sit about drinking tea all day. Not like some."

And away he went.

• • •

"How much are we paying these people?" Mr. Beeston said, as soon as he was back at the Department of Economies with his jarful of ghost under his arm. "These slackers at this Ministry of Ghosts?"

"I still haven't been able to find out yet, sir," Mrs. Peeve said. "The Human Resources Office says it can't find their records."

"Then what have they done with them?"

"They think they might have been accidentally filed away in the archives when they moved premises last year."

"Oh, wonderful," Mr. Beeston said (meaning, of course, quite the opposite). "So, what about employment records and past occupations? They've all been misfiled in the archives, too, have they?"

"That's what they seem to be saying, sir."

"Disgraceful," Mr. Beeston said. "Does anyone do any proper work here apart from me . . . and your good self, too, of course, Mrs. Peeve?"

"Well . . ."

"Never mind that for now. Let me have the files as soon as they turn up, and in the meantime, send this jar to the Medical Research Laboratories, will you? But tell them they'll need to examine it in the isolation room— the glass one, with the glass walls, floor, and ceiling."

Mrs. Peeve looked at the jar. "What is in here, sir?"

"A ghost, Mrs. Peeve. A ghost."

Mrs. Peeve took an abrupt step backward. "A ghost?"

"Allegedly a ghost. But I wouldn't be afraid of it. Because you know what I really think is in there, Mrs. Peeve?"

"What, sir?"

"Nothing! There's a big load of nothing in there, and those people at the Ministry of Ghosts are tricking me. But, just to be on the safe side, this jar shall only be opened under controlled conditions."

"Conditions are always best when they're controlled," Mrs. Peeve agreed. She peered into the jar to see if she could make the ghost out. "There seems to be something visible, Mr. Beeston, some sort of . . . smear of liquid . . . oily looking, perhaps."

"Condensed ghost, so I am told, Mrs. Peeve."

"Oh. Well, I've heard of condensed milk, but never—"

"No. And you are not alone. A jar of condensed ghost is also a new one to me. But we shall see, Mrs. Peeve. I shall have this examined as soon as possible. And if there isn't a ghost in there, then that Ministry is up for the chopping block. Meanwhile, any chance of getting a cup of tea, Mrs. Peeve?"

There was. And unlike Mrs. Scant's tea, Mrs. Peeve's tea actually turned up. Then she called the Medical Research Laboratories.

"They say the isolation room won't be ready for a few days, Mr. Beeston. They've got someone in there at the moment suffering from something contagious."

"And what disease is that exactly?"

"Not quite sure, sir. I didn't catch what they said."

"Can't be that contagious then."

"Pardon?"

"Nothing. All right, this jar of ghost can do as a paperweight for now," Mr. Beeston said, and he moved it to sit on top of some files on his desk. Mrs. Peeve stared at the jar again.

"I thought I saw something move just then," she said.

"Did you? Are you sure? Did you really?"

"Or, then again . . . maybe I didn't."

21
THE (AWFUL) TRUTH

Thruppence Coddley and Tim Legge tried everything. Whatever efforts they had made before, they now doubled them. It was only a matter of days, they knew, before that ruthless Mr. Beeston would be back—probably in a bad temper at having been deceived and fooled with an empty jar containing no more than a squirt of fish oil. And this time he would close the Ministry down forever, without hope of reprieve.

So they spent every free minute on their hunt for ghosts. Armed with trapping equipment, with incantations and spells, with candles and potions and small tinkling bells and other such lures, they tried to catch one.

They went back to St. Bindle's Church graveyard; they searched the crypt; they were nearly interrupted again by Reverend Reggie Mangle, but again they eluded him. They wandered down to the pet cemetery and tried there, for a ghost is a ghost, after all, whether human or animal.

They went to the undertaker's and waited until a hearse came along.

"It'll still be fresh," Tim said. "So we'll have a good chance of nabbing it."

And while the deceased was being unloaded, they hid in a doorway and muttered their spells, taken verbatim from Grimes and Natterly's *Manual of Ghost Hunting*. Yet, though they didn't step poorly or say a word out of place, no ghost appeared.

"It's hopeless," Tim then said. "Where have they all gone? Where are all the ghosts?"

"I don't know," Thruppence said. "But wherever they are, they're not around here."

So they caught a bus and tried elsewhere, and odd looks they got, too, from the bus driver and from their fellow passengers when they climbed aboard the No. 23 with their backpacks full of ghost-hunting equipment— with their bell, their books, their candles, and another large glass jar with a special stopper.

They went to distant cemeteries, to places reputed to be haunted, to old battlefields, to famous spots where un-happy lovers had leapt to their unfortunate ends, to the sites of ancient disasters, to any likely place where spirits might choose to dwell. But nothing. Not one small ghost to show for all their trouble.

Heavy-hearted and weary of foot, they returned home empty-handed and with an empty jar, yet again.

"It's no good," Tim said. "We're just going to have to tell them that we can't find anything. But we've done our best, and you can't do more than that, can you?"

"No, but it's such a shame. I've gotten to like them all," Thruppence said. "I'd feel terrible if they lost their jobs and the Ministry was closed down."

"Well, that inspector guy's going to find out what's really in that jar sooner or later."

"Okay. Let's go over and see them tomorrow afternoon and tell them that we've tried our best, but it's not going to work. At least it'll give them a chance to prepare for the worst."

So home they went: Tim to The Legge Works, and Thruppence to Good Coddley's Fish Shop.

"And not a word to anyone, Tim," Thruppence warned, as they parted. But the warning was unnecessary. They had come so far and had not told a soul the secret of what they were doing.

They entered their houses and went up to their rooms, as silent and as stealthy . . . as ghosts.

• • •

It was on the following afternoon when the whole thing unraveled—the great pity and, in some ways, the huge horror of it became clear. The dreadful facts revealed themselves, in all their bitter pathos and desperation.

But, for now, Tim Legge slept peacefully in his bed, and Thruppence Coddley slept soundly in hers, and neither of them dreamed that tomorrow they would meet a ghost—many ghosts; ghosts aplenty.

More ghosts than any reasonable person would care to see ever.

And these ghosts would come to haunt them for the rest of their lives.

• • •

It was Thruppence who realized it first. She and Tim were in Mr. Copperstone's office on the following afternoon. They had gone there immediately after school.

"Maybe we should give them back all the money that they've paid us," Thruppence said as they went. "I haven't spent any of mine yet. Have you?"

"No," Tim said. "Funnily enough, I haven't. I thought when we first got these jobs that I'd be hitting the stores big time, but I just haven't bothered somehow. I think the job's been better than the money, if you know what I mean."

They agreed that since they had been unsuccessful in their quest, they'd return at least a portion of their wages to Mr. Copperstone—after deducting a small amount for travel expenses and snacks.

But Mr. Copperstone would not hear of it.

They were all assembled in his office: Thruppence and Tim and Mr. Copperstone himself, and Miss Rolly and Mr. Gibbings and, of course, Mrs. Scant and—on this occasion—even Boddington the cat was present, curled up and asleep under a chair.

"I'm sorry, Mr. Copperstone," Tim began. "But Thruppence and I feel that we've let you down."

"Oh, no, no. No, no, no."

"Even with the extra week, we've not been able to find a ghost for you—"

"But you tried . . . you did try."

"We just wanted to warn you that, no doubt, that Beeston guy will soon find out the jar he was faked out with is empty, and then, well . . ."

"Yes. He'll be back—and the Ministry will be at an end."

A heavy silence filled the room, as heavy as those old Persian carpets lying on the floor; as heavy as the ancient filing cabinets stacked against the wall.

"What will become of us?" Mrs. Scant murmured. "Where shall we go?"

"The Ministry . . ." Mr. Gibbings began, and he was barely able to complete the phrase, "of Sewage . . ."

Thruppence looked at them. They all seemed so sad. For things to come to an end like this, for there to be such a parting of the ways . . . and then, yes, just then, as her eyes roamed around the room, taking in the wood paneling, the heavy flock wallpaper, the mirror on the wall, the dark paintings of illustrious forebears who had held Mr. Copperstone's job before him, the framed certificates in italic handwriting, the Japanese screen in a corner, the pencils, the pens, the old inkwell, the stack of parchment paper . . .

Her eyes swiveled. Then they swiveled back.

Her heart seemed to stop. Her whole body grew cold. Her mind filled with horror and terror. And she reached out, unnoticed by Mr. Copperstone, Mrs. Scant, Miss Rolly, or Mr. Gibbings, and she seized Tim Legge's hand, and she held it so tight that her nails dug into his flesh.

"Thruppence—"

"Tim, I think we ought to go now—"

"Must you? So soon?" Mr. Copperstone said.

"You've not had any tea," Mrs. Scant said.

"You've only just arrived," Mr. Gibbings said.

"Aren't we going to try and make another plan?" Miss Rolly said.

Thruppence's fear abated. She swallowed, and she forced herself to talk normally, as if nothing was amiss and everything was as it had always been.

"Yes, of course," she said. "We'll make another plan. Tim and I will make another plan, and we'll be back to see you tomorrow."

"Yeah, but . . ." Tim began. Thruppence squeezed his hand again, and Tim knew that something was up—only what?—and he fell silent.

"We'll be back tomorrow," Thruppence said again. "And I think we're going to have some news for you. Yes, I really think we are. So, come on, Tim, let's go now."

Before Tim could object, they were away, out of the office and hurrying down the stairs.

Mr. Copperstone looked somewhat perplexed.

"Why did they rush off so suddenly?" he said. "Does anyone know?"

But nobody seemed to.

The door of the Ministry closed behind them, and they were out on the street in the cool afternoon air.

"Thruppence—"

"Not here. Keep walking. Quickly. Around the corner. We can stop then, and I'll tell you."

"Thruppence . . ."

She all but ran, and Tim hurried to keep up with her. Then, safely at the end of Bric-a-Brac Street and around the corner onto Nick-Nack Street, Thruppence stopped by a lamp post to get her breath, and Tim caught her up.

"Thruppence, why did you leave like that? And why did you almost pull my hand off? What's the matter with you? You look like you've seen a ghost."

"I have," Thruppence said. "And so have you."

"No, I haven't. When?"

"You have, Tim. We've both been seeing them. We've been seeing them for a long time. We just didn't realize."

"What? What are you going on about? What ghost?"

"It's not one ghost, Tim. It's four."

"Four? What do you mean?"

"Up in Mr. Copperstone's office just now. I happened to glance in the mirror. I saw you, I saw me . . . the others—they don't have reflections. They're ghosts, Tim. Mr. Copperstone, Mrs. Scant, Miss Rolly, and Mr. Gibbings—every single one of them. They're ghosts."

Tim stood, open-mouthed, staring at her. "Oh my . . . We could have been . . . You mean we . . .? But what are we going to do, Thruppence? What are we going to do?"

But that was a question to which there was no easy or immediate answer.

22
NAMES AND DATES

They sat together in the churchyard of St. Bindle's. It seemed like an appropriate place to go—quiet, out of the way, a place they were unlikely to be disturbed. They perched on the edge of an old grave, which had a stone frame surrounding it as if it were some horizontal picture.

"It explains it all, of course, doesn't it?" Thruppence said.

"Does it?" Tim answered, looking doubtful.

"Well, it explains a lot."

"Such as?"

"Their clothes, for one thing. They're so old-fashioned."

"And what about the cat?" Tim said.

"I think the cat's a ghost, too."

"Can you have ghostly cats?"

"I don't see why not."

"Well, I suppose you don't have to worry about cat litter."

"No, Tim. Though I would have thought that would be the least of your worries."

216

"I wonder why they never moved on," Tim said. "I wonder why they're all still hanging around, haunting the Ministry."

"Only they know the answer to that," Thruppence said. "If anyone. But even if they do know doesn't mean they'll tell us. I don't even know if they realize they are ghosts."

"You don't think they know?"

"Or they do know—or suspect—but they won't face up to it."

Tim stretched out his legs. He was starting to feel quite at home in the small cemetery in some ways. It had become one of his favorite places. "They all must have worked there, I suppose."

"Of course," Thruppence said. "But it must have been at least a hundred years ago. Even more."

"Yes, those clothes of theirs are pretty old-fashioned," Tim said.

"Eveything is," Thruppence reminded him. "Not just the clothes. The old pens on the desks, that ancient type-writer. And those telephones. You never see telephones like that now. Except in a museum."

"But what I don't understand," Tim said, "is how they *do* things."

"Do things?" Thruppence repeated. "What things?"

"Everything," Tim said. "If they're ghosts then they can't pick things up, can they? They might look solid, but they're not. Their hands should just pass through every-thing. So how did they open the door? How did they write the notice saying 'Weekend Boy Wanted'?"

"Or Weekend Girl," Thruppence reminded him.

"Yes, well, how did they do that?"

"Because ghosts can move things around, can't they? Just by will. Because we never saw them actually open the door, did we? The door would just seem to open and there was Mrs. Scant or whoever. And it looked like they had opened the door with their hand and just released the handle. But we never actually saw them touch anything. Did we?"

"No. I suppose not," Tim conceded. "But I wonder why they never moved on? What did they want to stay here for? What do they actually do all day? And what happens to them at night?"

"We'll have to ask them," Thruppence said. "That's what we'll have to do."

Tim looked at her, shocked. "You mean—go back there?"

"Yes."

"But they're ghosts!"

"So?"

"But, they're ghosts, Thruppence. Ghosts!"

"But they're very nice ghosts, aren't they? And friendly. They've never done us any harm."

"No, maybe not, but—"

"And they're not scary at all."

"Well, no, they weren't when we didn't know they were ghosts, when we thought they were just a bit crazy but alive. But now we do know—"

"Tim, we promised to help them."

"Yes, I know, but—"

"And a promise is a promise."

"Maybe so. But I don't see—"

"And if that Mr. Beeston comes back once he discovers that jar is empty, well, he'll close the place down. And then where will they go? They'll have nowhere to haunt."

"Well, they can haunt somewhere else. Like that dumpster down the street."

"You can't expect four ghosts and a cat to haunt a tiny, cramped, dirty old dumpster. Not when they're used to a whole building."

"Yeah, but wait! Thruppence, that Mr. Beeston can't close the place down now."

"Why not?"

"Because he said he'd close the Ministry down if they couldn't produce a ghost. But they can. Four of them."

"Tim, I somehow don't think he's going to see it that way. I wonder . . ."

Thruppence suddenly got to her feet.

"What are you doing? Where are you going?" Tim said.

"I have an idea. Come and help."

"To do what?"

Thruppence was already walking among the gravestones.

"You take that side. I'll take this. Try and make out the names, and don't miss any."

Thruppence was the first to find what they were looking for. "Tim! Here! Look!"

And there it was—overgrown and covered in moss— an old, leaning memorial with a name on it:

JEREMIAH JARVIS COPPERSTONE
1839–1917
HE HAS GONE UNIVERSAL

"It must be him," Thruppence said. "Old Mr. Copperstone. I'm sure it's him. I'm sure."

"And look here," Tim said, pointing to another overgrown grave close by.

OLIVE GLADYS SCANT
1850–1920
SHE HAS GONE TO A BETTER PLACE

"Mind you, I don't know that she ever did actually go to a better place," Tim said. "She never left the Ministry of Ghosts, did she? She just went back and continued with her job."

After some searching, they found two more graves: one for Virginia Petunia Rolly and one for Arnold Peregrine Gibbings.

The first stone said that Miss Rolly had "given her life for the greater cause."

"What cause was that, I wonder?" Tim said. But Thruppence did not know, either, and just shrugged.

While under the name of Arnold Peregrine Gibbings were his dates and then the words: HE JUST PINED AWAY.

"Well, that's weird," Tim said. "I wonder what he pined away for?"

"Only one way to find out," Thruppence said.

"And what's that?"

"We'll need to go and ask him. But I think we have to be careful, Tim. Because I don't think they fully realize they are ghosts. And if we don't break the news to them gently . . ."

"What?"

"The shock could easily kill them."

"Um, Thruppence . . ."

"What?"

"I don't think that's a thing we have to worry about, to be honest."

"Oh . . . no. Maybe not. But all the same . . . we have to do it with tact."

• • •

The results that came back from the laboratory did not put Mr. Beeston in a good mood. Mr. Beeston was rarely in a good mood. He had possibly forgotten what a good mood looked like. But the news was not designed to refresh his memory.

"Herring oil!" he said in disgust. "You see this report, Mrs. Peeve? Nothing in that jar at all except a few drops of herring oil. Ghosts, indeed! They tell you you've got a ghost in a jar, and what have you really got? Herring oil. Well, they've gone too far this time. Far too far. I am going to pay another visit to this so-called Ministry of Ghosts and tell them it's time to pack their bags and to head for the Department of Sewage. I might even be recommending disciplinary action for all of them."

"Yes, Mr. Beeston," Mrs. Peeve said, holding a file of documents she had recently obtained from the Human Resources Office. "The only thing is . . ."

"The only thing is what, Mrs. Peeve? Because it seems to me that whenever I have set my course to follow some bold stroke of action, all I hear from my staff is: 'The only thing is . . .'"

Mrs. Peeve put the document folder down on his desk.

"It's the report you asked for, sir. About the four employees at the Ministry of Ghosts."

"Well?"

"None of them are on the payroll, sir."

"None of them?"

"Not one, sir. I've gone back over fifty years, and not one of any of those names is presently employed by the Ministry."

"But they must be."

"There aren't any records, sir."

"But . . . that's impossible. There's some mistake."

"Possibly, sir. But as far as Human Resources is concerned, the Ministry of Ghosts fell into disuse back in 1919. It seems that the place was forgotten about and the premises never adapted for anything else."

"This is just incompetence, Mrs. Peeve," Mr. Beeston said. "Not yours, plainly. It's those people at Human Resources. Of course, the Ministry is still operating. I've been there myself. I've seen the place. I've talked to the staff. Ridiculous. Get them to look at it again and to research it properly this time."

"Very well, sir."

"And while they're doing that, I shall get myself over to this Ministry, and I shall start by giving them a piece of my mind and finish by sending them to the Sewage Department. Apart from that old fool Copperstone, who's well past being useful. He can go on the scrapheap."

Fitting the deed to the word, Mr. Beeston gathered up the necessary forms for the redeployment and the retiring of staff, put them into his briefcase, and headed for the door.

23
HUGS AFTER ALL

The bell rang, and then the knocker banged. The old clock in the hallway struck the half hour. Mrs. Scant seemed to float along the corridor. She came to the door, reached out her hand, made a twisting motion, and the door swung open, perfectly silent now, with all its creaking gone.

"Our intrepid ghost hunters!" she said. "Do come in. Mr. Copperstone is up in his office, as always. Have you maybe brought us some good news today?"

Tim and Thruppence looked at each other.

"Well, yes . . . in a sense . . ." Tim said.

"And in a sense, no," Thruppence said. "But we do think we may have found some ghosts."

"Oh, you've found some? That's marvelous. Then we're saved. Have you brought them with you?" Mrs. Scant said, delighted. "Oh, wait until I tell Mr. Copperstone, and Miss Rolly and Mr. Gibbings!" She called out in a loud voice, "Good news, everyone! Good news! The Ministry is saved! Our hunters have found us a ghost!"

"It's not that simple, actually—" Thruppence tried to explain. But doors were already banging, and faces were appearing. Mr. Copperstone looked down from the top of the stairs.

"All come up to my office," he said. "Please, everyone come up. We must all hear this marvelous news together."

So, with heavy hearts and footsteps, Tim and Thruppence ascended the staircase, and they both noted, as they did so, that Mrs. Scant's rapid footsteps made no sound at all.

It was weird to be walking alongside a ghost.

"Come in, come in. So, it's good news then? Just in the nick of time, too, I think. That Beeston fellow could return at any moment. But if we have a real live ghost to show him, well, that will prove we were right all along. Yes, that will soon send him on his way. And the Ministry can continue with its good work indefinitely. Please, sit down."

Tim and Thruppence sat uncomfortably on two chairs. The others stood, watching expectantly.

"So . . . so where is it?" Mr. Copperstone asked. "I don't see a jar or anything—so where did you catch it? How did you catch it? Can we get a look at it? Where is this ghost?"

Thruppence shifted on her chair.

"Go on." Tim nudged her. "You tell them."

"Well, the thing is, Mr. Copperstone," Thruppence began, "we're about to tell you something that may come as quite a shock to you—to all of you. So, please don't be upset."

"But why should we be upset? You're bringing us good news, are you not? Found a ghost, you said."

"Four ghosts, actually," Tim said. "Well, five even."

"Five! Five ghosts! How splendid! How wonderful. So, where are they? What are their names? It's just, I don't see you . . . carrying anything."

"Mr. Copperstone . . . Mrs. Scant . . . Miss Rolly . . . Mr. Gibbings . . ." Thruppence said. "I'm so sorry to have to tell you this, as you clearly don't seem to realize—or you do, but you haven't fully accepted it—and please don't take this the wrong way . . . but the ghosts are . . . well, they're you."

"You and the cat," Tim added, "makes five."

Silence. Cold, frozen silence. Mr. Copperstone's mouth moved, but no sound came out. Mrs. Scant's hand made a vague, kettle-pouring gesture, but what it was meant to convey only she knew. Miss Rolly took a handkerchief—a ghost of a handkerchief—from her skirt pocket, and she held it to her eye. And Mr. Gibbings, his eyes were fixed upon Miss Rolly as if he feared for her and did not wish to see her harmed.

"Please go and look in the mirror," Thruppence said. "You don't have reflections. None of you. If you look, there's nothing there."

"I don't know if you've ever read *101 Things You Never Knew About the Paranormal*," Tim said. "It's in your library. And it says in there . . ."

But they weren't listening. They were clustered around the mirror, all four of them peering into it as if the mysteries of the universe would be revealed in its silvery depths.

"She's right," Mr. Copperstone said. "She's quite correct. I'm not there, am I? I'm not there. I'm nowhere to be seen. Oh dear. What a situation. I shall have to sit down. Oh dear, oh dear."

Why Mr. Copperstone needed to sit down when he was a ghost that—though solid-looking—had no weight at all was hard to understand. Even he didn't really know why he needed to sit down. But it was what he did.

"H-how long have we been like this?" Mr. Gibbings asked. "Do you happen to know?"

"About a hundred years. Around about that," Thruppence said. "You're all buried down at St. Bindle's, in the graveyard."

"Are we?" Mrs. Scant said. "All of us together? How friendly. That's nice."

"Didn't any of you realize?" Thruppence said. "Didn't you suspect? Didn't you know? I mean, what do you do here? When evening comes, when the working day is over and you can't really go on pretending any more, what do you do?"

"Do?" Mr. Copperstone looked confused. "Well, I . . . that is . . . when half-past five comes . . . I go . . . well, home . . . I thought . . . or maybe . . . but then I'm always here again, first thing in the morning, sitting at my desk and ready to continue with things . . ."

"And I come in then, don't I, Mr. Copperstone, and I say: 'Cup of tea for you, sir?'"

"Indeed you do, Mrs. Scant. And very grateful I am for it and very appreciative, too. For no one makes a cup of tea like Mrs. Scant, only—"

"I know. The tea never comes anymore, does it, sir."

"I couldn't drink it, even if it did, Mrs. Scant . . ."

"No more than I could, Mr. Copperstone. Our tea-drinking days are long gone."

"But the thought's still there, Mrs. Scant."

"Yes, sir. The thought is always there."

Silence again. Sad, horrible silence.

Thruppence broke it by reaching into her pocket, taking out, and unfolding a piece of paper.

"I wrote down all your dates," she said. "You died first, Mr. Copperstone. Why did you come back? Why didn't you just move on to wherever it is that people go when they die?"

Mr. Copperstone's sad face suddenly brightened. "Why did I come back? For Mrs. Scant, of course. No other reason. So I could see her every day and be here in the same building. How could I move on when Mrs. Scant was here? My own marriage was not a good one, but I grew so fond of Mrs. Scant."

"Oh, Mr. Copperstone," she said. "I never knew it was mutual. I never knew you cared for me the way I do for you."

"Of course I care, Mrs. Scant. Of course I do."

"Then you should have said so. Because when Mr. Scant died, I never wanted to see him again—horrible man that he was. But once a widow, I always hoped that you might, perhaps . . ."

"But then you died, Mrs. Scant, some three years after Mr. Copperstone," Thruppence said.

"And I came back here looking for him, and here he was, still at his desk. So I just continued everything as normal. I mean, the place had been closed down really. But . . . well . . . it didn't seem to make any difference."

"And you, Miss Rolly? You died very young," Thruppence said.

"I was a suffragette," Miss Rolly said. "One weekend I went on a demonstration—fighting for women's votes. I was arrested. So I went on hunger strike and—"

"She was so brave," Mr. Gibbings said. "So steely minded and so tremendously brave . . ."

"So I had to come back," Miss Rolly said, "to keep up the fight."

"No need, Miss Rolly," Thruppence said. "We've got the vote. We've had it for years and years and years."

"Yes, well, to be honest, that wasn't the only reason . . ." Mr. Gibbings spoke up. "I flatter myself that perhaps Miss Rolly . . . maybe came back . . . for me."

"Oh, Arnold!" Miss Rolly exclaimed. "You knew?"

"Just as I came back for her," he said. "For when she went on the hunger strike and died for the cause, well, it hit me badly, Miss Rolly, it hit me badly."

"It did?"

"I just went into decline. I couldn't eat; I couldn't sleep; I could only think of you. It broke my heart, Miss Rolly, that you were gone. And a broken heart is a thing you can die of. And that was why I came back to haunt the Ministry, so as to mend my broken heart."

"And is it . . . is it mended, Arnold?" Miss Rolly asked.

"It is, Virginia," Mr. Gibbings said. "As long as you are here."

Thruppence Coddley rose abruptly to her feet.

"Now stop it!" she snapped. "Just stop it! Stop it, all of you. Because if you don't stop it . . . if you don't stop all this right now . . . I shall probably . . . start to cry."

Tim Legge looked up at her, and he reached to his pocket for a tissue. "I'm crying already," he said. "It's worse than *Bambi*. Will you give me a hug, Thruppence?" he said. "I know we said no hugs ever, but given the circumstances . . ."

"Of course I will, Tim," she said. "Gladly. But you'll have to give me one, too."

The ghosts looked at the living, and the living looked at the ghosts. But it wasn't as if they were different beings—it was more that they were all part of the one, same thing, of life and of losing it and of the feelings everyone must have and the happinesses and sadnesses that everyone must go through.

"Oh dear," Mr. Copperstone said. "Oh dear. What to do, huh? What to do? What is a ghost to do? We could have gone on forever here if it hadn't been for that awful man, that horrible Beeston fellow. If only he had just left us in peace. If only he had never been born."

But Mr. Beeston had been born. He had started off as a baby, and he had developed into the hatchet man at the Department of Economies.

And right now he was standing at the front door of the Ministry of Ghosts, and he held the door knocker in his strong right hand.

He bashed it hard against the door.

24
MR. BEESTON'S LAST VISIT

Mr. Beeston was rather surprised to see who opened the door to him. It quite took the wind from his wrath-filled sails. He had been ready to go on the attack from the first creak of the hinges. But not only was there no creak; there was no one to shout at. There were just these two, well, children. And what were they doing there at the Ministry of Ghosts at that hour in the morning? Surely they should have been at . . . well . . . school, for example?

Mr. Beeston couldn't have known that it was a school holiday. But even if he had known, it would not have fully relieved his perplexity. What were two children—a boy with hair sticking up everywhere and a girl who smelled of fresh strawberries—doing behind the counter (so to speak) of a government department?

Children and the civil service did not mix. The civil service was a serious business, whereas children, alas, as Mr. Beeston knew from harsh experience, could be inclined to frivolity.

Mr. Beeston shifted the big glass jar that he was carrying under his arm into a more comfortable position.

The glass jar had a Post-it note stuck to it. Written on the note was: "Exhibit one."

There appeared to be no exhibit two.

He cleared his throat and he came straight to the point. "Who the heck are you?" he said.

"Thruppence Coddley," Tim Legge said, indicating his companion.

"And Timothy Legge, my colleague," Thruppence said, pointing at Tim. "Charmed, I'm sure."

Mr. Beeston was far from charmed. He was more along the lines of perplexed.

"And what are you two doing here? This is a government department. Why aren't you at school?"

"School holiday. And we work here on a part-time basis," Thruppence said.

"Doing what?"

"Ghost hunting," she smiled.

Mr. Beeston turned a very strange color. It was sort of gray, but kind of red, too, with hints of purple.

"I wish to see Mr. Copperstone," he said. "Where is he?"

"He asked us to show you in and to take you upstairs," Thruppence said. "Please—this way."

With a pleasant expression, she invited Mr. Beeston to enter. Once in, Tim closed the door behind him.

"Would you care to put your big jam jar down?" Thruppence said. "It looks rather heavy."

"Jam jar! This happens to be a ghost jar. And I am holding onto it. It is exhibit number one in the Ministry of Ghosts's Hall of Shame!"

"Oh dear," Thruppence said. "That sounds serious."

"There was supposed to be a condensed ghost in here!" Mr. Beeston said. "But all that's really in here is herring oil."

"I can't think where that could have come from," Tim said, with an admirably straight face and a wink in Thruppence's direction.

"I'm sure Mr. Copperstone will be able to explain everything. Please. This way," Thruppence said again. "Oh, and by the way, may I ask who's calling?"

Mr. Beeston's appearance went farther along the color chart in the direction of puce.

"Who's calling? Me! I am! That's who's calling. Me, standing here. You just tell 'em it's Beeston and that'll be all they need to know. It'll have them quaking in their shoes!"

"Someone's certainly going to be quaking in their shoes . . ." Tim whispered to Thruppence. Mr. Beeston did not hear him.

Up they went to Mr. Copperstone's office. Thruppence tapped lightly on the door.

"Do come in. We're all here."

In they went. And there they were. Old Mr. Copperstone; not quite so old, but not really young Mrs. Scant; eternally young and fiery Miss Rolly; and youngish and slightly sad Mr. Gibbings.

"Ah. You're all here," Mr. Beeston correctly observed. "That's good, too, because I've got news for you. You won't be in this job for much longer. At least not a cushy one like you've had for years."

"Mr. Beeston," Mr. Copperstone said graciously, "to what do we owe the pleasure of this visit? Please, do take a seat."

Beeston did. He sat straight-backed with the big jar on his knee.

"Now then, Copperstone," he said. "First off, what are these two doing here?" He indicated Tim and Thruppence.

"They are employed by the Ministry on a freelance, part-time basis," Mr. Copperstone said, "to hunt ghosts. It is well known—I refer you, if you have any doubts, to Grimes and Natterly's *Manual of Ghost Hunting*—that children have a peculiar sensitivity to and attraction for ghosts. I think it is on pages one-seven-five to one-seven-eight."

"Spare me the academic references," Beeston said. "The fact is they're too young to be working."

"Not at all," Mr. Copperstone said. "Why, my own brother was out to work at the age of seven. He had a job with the local coalman. He used to look after his horse."

Mr. Beeston held a hand up for silence.

"Enough!" he said. "That's all irrelevant anyway. It's all of no consequence. Not seeing that this Ministry is on the chopping block!"

"The chopping block?" Mr. Copperstone said.

"The chopping block?" Mrs. Scant repeated.

"The chopping block?" Miss Rolly said.

"The chipping block?" Mr. Gibbings said.

"No, the chopping block!" Mr. Beeston snapped.

"Sorry," Mr. Gibbings said. "I misheard."

"Now look, Copperstone. You had three months to find a ghost. You told me you'd gotten one. In this jar, you said. Well, I had it opened up in laboratory conditions—in a laboratory."

"Is that so?" Mr. Copperstone said.

"There was never any ghost in here. Never. All that's in here is some herring oil."

"Herring oil?"

"Herring oil, smeared around the inside to make it look like there was a ghost inside."

"Surely not?"

"Well, I'm not fooled by it. Not for a moment. In fact, you know what I think all this herring oil is, Copperstone? It's a red herring!"

"A red herring? So you believe that a herring is nothing but a red herring?"

"Don't play games with me, Copperstone. You had three months to justify the existence of this Ministry. You've had years and years before that in which to produce a ghost. Decades. Ages. Centuries. This place hasn't come up with one single ghost since it was founded in 1792! Well, enough already. The end has come, Copperstone. And by the powers vested in me, I now declare—"

"Excuse me . . ."

Mr. Beeston stopped in mid-flight. He glared at the girl who had interrupted him. "What?"

"We have found some ghosts."

Mr. Beeston sneered and laughed in a rather horrible way.

"Oh yes. More empty jars, is it? All smeared up with herring? Oh no. Once bitten, twice shy. You don't fool Beeston twice. Not with that same old trick."

"It's not a trick at all," Thruppence said. "Mr. Copperstone, please, if you would. If you'd care to give a demonstration?"

"Of course, my dear. My pleasure."

Mr. Copperstone stood up behind his desk. He smiled. He stepped forward, heading for the side of the room. He kept on walking. He came to the wall. He continued walking. The wall did not stop him. He walked right through it. He vanished completely from sight. Then he reappeared through one of the other walls.

"There, you see," he said to Mr. Beeston. "How was that?"

Mr. Beeston did not answer. He just sat on his chair, his lower lip hanging open and twitching slightly. Before the ability to speak returned to him, Mr. Gibbings stood up to show what he could do, and said, "How about this, too?"

He jumped on the spot. And when he landed, he went straight through the floor and disappeared. He reappeared a moment later, reentering from behind a picture.

Mr. Beeston had started to tremble.

"May I try, too?" Mrs. Scant said. "It looks like such fun."

She stood and walked up the wall, walked upside down along the ceiling, tightly gripping her skirts for modesty, dangled a while from the light fixtures, and then scampered back down the wall on the other side.

Mr. Beeston was, by this time, clutching at his chest.

"Oh me, too!" Miss Rolly said. "I want to try as well."

Not to be outdone by the others, she stretched herself out in all directions until she was about twelve feet tall and nine feet wide, and then she exploded into lots of different pieces and the pieces splattered all around the room, as if a can of paint had erupted. There were pieces of Miss Rolly everywhere, including on Mr. Beeston.

"Eeeech!" he yelled. "Get it off!"

Which she immediately did, and all the pieces reassembled, and there was Miss Rolly again, as trim and prim as ever.

"I don't know why I never did that before," she said. "There's something about exploding that really cheers you up."

The expression upon Mr. Beeston's face was now one of unmistakable horror. This, his eyes seemed to say, was the road to madness; this way insanity lay.

"There are plenty of other tricks we could probably manage," Mr. Copperstone magnanimously offered. "Would you care to see me get inside the inkwell?"

"Or I could turn myself into a spoon," Mrs. Scant said.

"How about I start levitating that chair you're sitting on?" Miss Rolly said. Mr. Beeston's chair began to rise, with him on it.

"No! Put me down!"

The chair bumped back to the floor.

"How about I turn myself into a pair of bagpipes?" Mr. Gibbings said. "It's absolutely no trouble. I can probably make all the noises as well."

Mr. Beeston did not take up his offer. He just sat and stared and tried his best to keep breathing.

"If you like, we could take possession of you for a couple minutes. I'm sure it will be an experience," Mr. Copperstone offered.

Before Mr. Beeston could refuse, Mr. Copperstone took possession of one of Beeston's legs and Mr. Gibbings took the other, while Miss Rolly and Mrs. Scant had an arm each.

It was a very odd feeling, having somebody else in your body, fighting for control of your limbs. Mr. Beeston did not like it at all.

"Go away," Mr. Beeston told them. "It's my body!" he yelled. "Get out of it!"

"Come now, don't be selfish," Mrs. Scant told him. "Room inside for a small one."

"You're anything but a small one."

"Bit bony, this elbow is," she said.

They ran him around the office, down the stairs, into the basement, up to the attic, around the landing, and back into the office again. They made him do handstands, somersaults, and several back flips. Then they dumped him down onto his chair again and made him bash himself lightly on his head with both hands, as though he were playing the bongos.

Finally, the ghosts left him and resumed their shapes and their seats.

"So there you have it," Thruppence said, as Mr. Beeston tried to understand what was happening to him. "You can't close the Ministry of Ghosts down now, can

238

you? Not for lack of ghosts. You've just seen four of them—"

Suddenly a ghostly cat appeared, and it sat on Mr. Beeston's head.

"Better make that five," Tim said.

"Get it off me!" Mr. Beeston screamed.

"Boddington. Come down from there," Mrs. Scant commanded. "Bad cat."

The cat hopped down. Mr. Beeston stood. The heavy glass jar he had brought was knocked over and rolled to the carpet. It rolled across the floor and came to rest by the leg of Mr. Copperstone's desk. The power of speech had all but gone from Mr. Beeston. Yet he managed to raise a hand, and he pointed at the adults in the room.

"You," he said. "And you. And you. And you." Then Mr. Beeston said, "Ahhhh!" several times over and over again. Then he fled. He crashed from the room and down the stairs and out of the front door and along Bric-a-Brac Street. He ran and ran for all he was worth until he came to the bus terminal, where, fortunately for him, a bus was waiting.

He banged on the door. The driver, who was on his break, beckoned him to wait. But Mr. Beeston just banged again until the door was opened and he could get on board.

"You all right?" the bus driver said, a little worried about being alone in the bus with such a passenger. "You look like you've seen a ghost."

Mr. Beeston reached out and gripped the driver by his arm. "You mean you've seen them, too?" he said.

The driver looked very uneasy.

"Plenty of seats at the back," he said. "Why don't you go and sit down?"

"Let's get going," Mr. Beeston said. "Soon as we can. Before they come for me!"

"Oh?" the driver said. "They're coming for you, are they? Well, don't you worry. I'll have a word with them if they do, and I'll tell them to leave you alone."

"Would you?" Mr. Beeston said. "I'd be so grateful. One of them exploded, you know. All over me. And then the cat sat on my head."

"Did he now?"

"And Copperstone threatened to get inside the ink-well."

"Well, no wonder you're upset," the driver said—for he was used to humoring difficult passengers, especially late at night when the pubs closed, though not so much during the day.

"I'm never going back there again," Mr. Beeston said. "It's a nightmare!"

"No, if I were you, sir, I'd try to forget about the whole thing. I'd just bury it, if I were you."

"Bury it," Mr. Beeston said. "Yes. Bury it all. Yes. You might be right."

25

THE END IS NIGH

Bury it all. Yes. Maybe that was right. Just move on to other matters; forget what had happened. Let all the weird and wonderful and inexplicable things in the world simply take care of themselves. And get on with your life, and enjoy what you could.

Tim Legge and Thruppence Coddley were in the churchyard at St. Bindle's, and they had brought flowers with them. They had bought them with their ghost-hunting earnings.

They carefully sought out four of the graves and tenderly laid flowers by each of them. The names on the graves were Copperstone, Scant, Rolly, and Gibbings. It had been many years since anyone had come with flowers or had mourned these passings. Many long, long years.

As they lay the flowers by the gravesides, Reverend Reggie Mangle came by and, intrigued by the sight of children placing flowers on ancient tombstones, he stopped to chat and to ask if they were in any way related to the long deceased and the dear departed. For it seemed to him that these people had left the world a long time ago, long before these children had been born.

"No, we're not related," Thruppence said. "We're more along the lines of . . . how would you describe it, Tim?"

"Friends," Tim said. "That's all. We're just friends."

Far from satisfying Reverend Mangle's curiosity, these replies only intensified it. Intrigued, he followed up with further questions until finally the children told him all. In many ways they were glad to, for it was a weight off their shoulders. To have to carry such knowledge around and not to be able to share it was quite a burden.

"Ghosts!" Reverend Mangle said, on first hearing. "Don't you worry. Bell, book, candle, and a splash of holy water! I'll soon have them shifted. I'll soon get rid of them for you. I've dealt with things like this before. It reminds me of my wrestling days, when I had a bout with The Phantom and he tried to chew my ear off—"

"No, no, please," Thruppence said. "We don't want to get rid of them. They're the nicest, kindest ghosts you could ever imagine. We just want them to be left in peace. They seem to like each other. They're happy together. We just want to make sure that they're never disturbed."

"I see. Yes. So, it's those four over at the Ministry, is it?"

"That's right," Tim said. "Plus the cat."

"You know, I thought there was something strange about that setup," Reverend Mangle said. "There was something odd about the place. And a chill in the rooms . . ."

"Well, as long as Mr. Beeston doesn't come back, they ought to be left in peace. So you won't hurt them, will you, Mr. Mangle?"

"My dear girl," the fearsome reverend said. "I wouldn't hurt a fly."

Nor would he. Not since the day he had seen the light.

• • •

Mr. Beeston never did come back. He returned to his office and summoned Mrs. Peeve to him.

"Just file all these papers, if you would, Mrs. Peeve," he said.

"The Ministry of Ghosts, sir? But I thought you intended to close the place with immediate effect."

"I've, um . . . changed my mind. More important matters to deal with. Just file it all away and forget about it."

"But, sir, I—"

"That'll be all, thank you, Mrs. Peeve. That'll be all."

And so it was. And so it may have remained forever. The ghosts continued to haunt the Ministry where they had once been employees and where they could not bear to leave, any more than they could bear to be parted from those they had loved—even if that affection had never been fully declared.

Every weekday morning they were at their desks. And Mrs. Scant continued to promise tea—tea that never did or ever would arrive. And Mr. Copperstone took forty winks. And Miss Rolly and Mr. Gibbings sat together during their lunch hours (of uneaten and nonexistent lunch) and talked much of the future and of women's rights and of greater equalities and of the brave new world that would one day come into being, even if not in their lifetimes.

In the evenings, all would seem to doze and to fall into slumber, and the Ministry was so quiet, so silent then, that it seemed the whole building was empty. It was so quiet you could have heard a distant tap drip, a spoon stir, a gnat sneeze.

But every now and again, real live visitors would appear. They had their own keys and they let themselves in. Tim Legge and Thruppence Coddley, growing up now but still coming to see their old friends the ghosts.

For a while their visits tailed off. Teenage years. Better things to do than to visit old folks and such.

But, as more years passed, the visits resumed. It was always nice to sit and to chat with the four ghosts, to hear firsthand accounts of the past.

One day, Thruppence Coddley and Tim Legge had news of their own. They were grown up now, and they had known each other so long and had grown so fond of each other that they felt they wanted to be together all the time. Just like Mr. Copperstone and Mrs. Scant. And Miss Rolly and Mr. Gibbings.

So, guess what? Guess what!

Yes. That's right. That's right.

And, in time again, Tim took over his father's business and Good Coddley's Fish Shop became Thruppence's affair. She worked hard, and she worked long hours. But she always smelled of fresh strawberries somehow. It was a wonder how she managed that.

Then a baby came along. And then another. The first called Jeremiah Jarvis Arnold Peregrine, after Mr. Copperstone and Mr. Gibbings; the second called Olive

Gladys Virginia Petunia, after Mrs. Scant and fiery Miss Rolly.

And that was how things could have stayed. But things never do stay the same forever. There is always change. It waits and it lurks around every corner, and it takes you by surprise.

Scaffolding appeared one morning outside of the Ministry of Ghosts. The brass plate was dull and tarnished again now and had been so for years. Thruppence had long since stopped polishing it. She felt anonymity was best. She and Tim were walking past. Young Jeremiah was toddling along beside her. Tim was pushing Olive in her stroller.

"Tim. Whatever's going on?"

They used their key and let themselves inside. The ghosts greeted them and were pleased to see the baby and young Jeremiah, and yet they looked worried, too.

"What's going on, Mr. Copperstone? What's the scaffolding for?"

"It seems that the building has been sold," Mr. Copperstone said. "It's been twenty years or more since that awful Beeston was here. He must have retired and someone new has taken over. They have realized that no one works here and nothing happens here anymore, and they have sold the place. There's a letter . . ."

The letter drifted over to Thruppence on a ghostly breeze. She read it and passed it to Tim.

"New offices? A fitness center? A sauna? A coffee shop?"

"Yes. It's going to be so noisy, isn't it? I don't know what we're going to do. I don't know where we're going to go."

"I do," Thruppence said. "We do, don't we, Tim?"

"That's right," Tim said. "There's only one place you can go."

"You mean back to the cemetery, I suppose," Mr. Copperstone said. "To move on to the afterlife. And maybe never to see each other again, ever, for all . . . all eternity."

Mrs. Scant stifled a ghostly sob.

"No," Thruppence said, indignantly. "Of course we don't mean that. You must come and live with us, naturally. You shall come and live with us."

"Oh, can we?" Mr. Copperstone said. "Can we really? Only, won't we frighten your children?"

But the children were so used to ghosts they weren't frightened at all. In fact, they were rather fond of them.

• • •

So that is what happened. There they were, and there they remained, and there they are to this day. They live with Thruppence and Tim.

They have their own little room with a television and a remote control that they can use by levitation, and in the winter the ghosts all hibernate up in the loft.

Sometimes, if both Tim and Thruppence have to be out, the ghosts keep an eye on the children. It's only ever for a few minutes. And they can usually levitate things out of danger should any trouble arise. They also house-sit for the family when they go on vacation and frighten off any burglars.

As for Reverend Mangle, he was moved to another parish. Before he left, he came around to say goodbye. In some ways he felt that the four ghosts should also move on and that it was his job to see they did.

But then, as Thruppence pointed out to him, if all people want to do is to be together and they do no one else any harm, then why not let them? Why break the spell? Why not just live and let live? You surely wouldn't begrudge people a little happiness, would you? When it took them so long to find it?

Reverend Mangle thought long and hard about that one—very long, and very hard.

Then, no, he said. He wasn't one to begrudge anybody a little happiness at all. Because that was what life was for—life and all eternity.

Live and let live, he agreed. Live and let live.

Then he said goodbye to Thruppence and to Tim and to their children, and to Mr. Copperstone and to Mrs. Scant and to Miss Rolly and to Mr. Gibbings and to Boddington, the pale shadow of a cat.

And then he was gone, away down the street. Vanished.

Like a ghost.

ABOUT THE AUTHOR

Alex Shearer was born in Wick, in the far North of Scotland. He has written several TV series, stage plays, radio plays, and comedy scripts. Moving into writing for children, his novels *Bootleg* and *The Greatest Store in the World* were adapted for television by the BBC, and his 2003 novel *The Speed of the Dark* was shortlisted for the Guardian Children's Fiction Prize. He has previously published *The Cloud Hunters* and *Sky Run* with Sky Pony Press, and he lives in Somerset and is married with two grown-up children.